Boy vs. Girl

Bismillah

Dedicated to all who work to inspire our youth

With special thanks to Humayrah, Aaminah,
Jannah, Sara, Sameer, Umm Abdur-Rahman,
Umm Ruqeyah and Umm Junayd -
this book is what it is because of you.

JANETTA OTTER-BARRY BOOKS

Boy vs Girl copyright © Frances Lincoln Limited 2010
Text copyright © Naima B Robert 2010

First published in Great Britain in 2010 and in the USA in 2011 by
Frances Lincoln Children's Books, 4 Torriano Mews,
Torriano Avenue, London NW5 2RZ

www.franceslincoln.com

British Library Cataloguing in Publication Data available on request

ISBN: 978-1-84780-150-0

Printed in Dongguan, Guangdong, China by South China
in December 2010

1 3 5 7 9 8 6 4 2

Na'ima B. Robert

F
FRANCES LINCOLN
CHILDREN'S BOOKS

Chapter 1

Good Intentions

Farhana stood in front of her full-length mirror and scrutinised her reflection. Her hair was loose, ready to be restrained in a regulation ponytail for school. But for now, it hung about her shoulders and down her back, straight, but not dead straight enough to be the height of fashion. Nothing a pair of ceramic straighteners wouldn't fix, though. All the hot Asian girls wore their hair dead straight nowadays – curls were so out.

She peered at her skin, smooth, the colour of a latte, with a hint of mocha. With her green eyes framed by long, dark eyelashes and full lips, guys often compared her to Aishwara Rai, the famous Bollywood actress. As if. Guys will say anything to get what they want.

Her school uniform sat loosely on her tall frame and skimmed her curves, just the way her mum liked it. No jumper bought two sizes too small for her, no skirts hitched up above the knee. Her version of the school uniform was just modest enough - what a decent Pakistani girl should look like, as Ammiji would say.

But as she adjusted her waistband her eyes flickered upwards, towards the white piece of fabric that was perched on the corner of the mirror. In the back of her mind, she could hear her Auntie Najma's voice: 'The *hijab* is a protection, Farhana, not an oppression. Your body, the beauty you've been blessed with, are your private property, not to be seen by just anyone. You're worth so much more than that.'

Farhana swallowed hard and reached for the *hijab*. She imagined herself folding it into a neat triangle, the edges precisely matched, lifting it over her head and bringing the two sides together under her chin, taking a pin and pinning it closed, drawing the two ends over her shoulders. Farhana in *hijab*. Did she dare?

But then she heard her mother's voice: 'Dressing modestly is enough – so many people go to extremes these days. Just look at your Auntie Najma! You don't need all this *hijab, jilbab, niqab* nonsense. For a start, it's not our culture and, while we are living here, we should try to blend in, not stand out. It gives the wrong impression, that Muslim women are oppressed. As long as you have faith in your heart, that's all you need.'

And she saw too, with absolute clarity, the shock on Shazia's face, the horror on Robina's, the weird looks from the other girls at school, the smirks from the guys down the town centre.

And then there was Malik. What would he say?

She shook her head. Of course she didn't dare. Not yet. Not today.

"Farhana! Faraz!" Her mother's voice came from downstairs. "Hurry up, you'll be late!"

Farhana grabbed her bag and scooped her books off her desk. She'd pack them properly later. "Coming, Ammiji!" she called down.

★ ★ ★

In his room across the hall, Farhana's twin brother Faraz was also getting ready for school. Born six minutes after his sister, he was later than her in most other things too. He had not yet put on his school shirt, and was standing in front of the mirror in a vest and school trousers. He had already spiked his hair with gel as he did every morning, after splashing cologne on to his neck and stubbly chin. He smiled inwardly when he thought of the beard that was trying to assert itself – he was a man already.

He turned and looked again at his upper arm, smooth, brown and muscular. All that time at the gym last year had paid off: he wasn't weedy any more. Then he thought of the needles, the blue ink, the stain that might soon appear there, and he winced.

Could he really go through with it?

Things he had heard since childhood, in *madressah*, in conversations between his father and the brothers at the mosque, flew through his mind: tattoos, *haram*, forbidden in Islam. 'There is to be no change in the creation of Allah …' Wasn't that what his Auntie Najma had said? He bit his lip.

Then he remembered Skrooz's voice, smooth as honey, with an edge as sharp as a switchblade. 'All the lads have it, Fraz. This symbol is powerful, blud, it commands respect, wherever you go. But not everyone can get it, y'know.

You have to *earn* it, see? And you...' He had pointed at him, nodding his head, looking at him sideways. 'You're well on your way, son, well on your way. Just a few more little errands for me and you'll wear the badge too.'

Faraz felt his heart expand in his chest. It felt good to see the sly looks of respect that came his way nowadays. Maybe one tattoo was worth it? Just the one...

He heard his mother calling him and he shouted down to her. "I'm there, Ammiji, I'm there!"

He grabbed the clean, pressed school shirt that his mother had hung up for him the night before and shrugged it on. A clean shirt was as far as he would go to appease his mother – she could forget the tie though. Only losers wore ties at his school.

Another call from downstairs and he bolted out of the door.

★ ★ ★

"I spoke to *Imam* Shakir last night," said the twins' father, Mahmood, as he peered at the morning paper over his breakfast.

"Did he say when he thought Ramzan would

be?" Their mother, Uzma, was lifting fried eggs on to two plates, supervising the toaster, waiting for the kettle to boil.

"He reckons next Monday," answered Mahmood, sipping his hot, sweet tea, "but they will wait to hear the news from Pakistan before announcing it."

"D'you think we'll start fasting with everyone else in the UK this year, Dad?" Farhana poured herself a glass of juice and sat down.

"Ah, get us a drink, sis," Faraz said over his shoulder as he sat programming his iPod.

"Sure, lazybones," she said, scowling good-naturedly. Why did he always have to be waited on? Honestly, men!

Uzma, the twins' mother, gazed fondly at this exchange between her two children. Farhana and Faraz had been born after six years of marriage - a lifetime in her mother's eyes - and there had been no more children after that. This certainly wasn't what she had imagined when she had first made that trip over from Karachi as a new bride, all those years ago.

Alhamdulillah, her parents had chosen well: Mahmood, her cousin, was a good man, she couldn't fault him and, all in all, she was content. She had a girl *and* a boy and they were good kids, respectful and well-behaved. She didn't worry about them going off the rails and doing anything crazy, like some of her friends' children... Even Pakistanis weren't safe from the corruption that filled the media, it seemed.

She shuddered slightly when she remembered the riots that had taken place a few years earlier, riots that had spilled over into her life when a gang of youths had looted their little newsagent's shop. She remembered thanking God that her Faraz wasn't old enough to be involved. He had still been an awkward lad in glasses at the time. Not that she ever worried about him getting into that sort of thing. Not her Faraz. He had always been the soft one, the tender one, the one who came to give you a hug for no reason, who could cry over a beautiful recitation of the *Qur'an*.

Farhana was the tough one, the brainy one, who wanted reasons and explanations for everything. Uzma knew that it was meant to be the other way round but she couldn't deny their true characters, any more than their father could accept that Faraz was not a macho sportsman like he had been. She poured her husband another cup of tea and turned her thoughts to Ramadan.

"Well, it depends, Farhana," Mahmood was saying. "The mosque will want to follow Pakistan, as they always have, so we'll just do what they do."

Farhana was always baffled by the debates about the start of Ramadan – about whether the moon had been sighted or not, and by whom, and in which country. It seemed simple enough: if the new moon was seen, the new month in the lunar calendar had begun: time to start fasting. It didn't stop people arguing about it, though....

She bit into her toast thoughtfully. In a few days, they wouldn't be eating at this time. The kitchen would be clean and silent, no plates or cups on the table, no sizzling frying pan. That would all have been cleared away after *sehri*, the meal they ate before dawn, while it was still dark. It would only come to life again in the afternoon, when they started to prepare the food before *iftar*, the evening meal to break their fast, at sunset.

Farhana smiled. She was looking forward to Ramadan this year. Something inside her said that this year would be different from all the others.

I'm going to make a change, she thought to

herself, and her smile broadened.

Faraz, too, had Ramadan on his mind. He had tried to fast last year but there was too much going on, too many distractions. He had given up halfway through, although his parents didn't know. It was easy enough to get a bite to eat down the town centre where his parents rarely ventured – there weren't too many Asians there and the shops stayed open all day.

But this year, he planned to do it properly. He was sixteen, after all. He didn't need the stubbly chin to remind him that he was a man now, at least according to their faith. *Time to fix up.*

Chapter 2

Inspired

There was no rest for anyone on Saturday. Even the twins didn't get to have their traditional lie-in. Ammiji was in their rooms, opening the curtains with a flourish, before 9:30am.

"Come on, up, you two," she said briskly. "Ramzan's coming - we've got lots to do!"

First, there was the house to get in order: cleaning, dusting, airing the mattresses, dealing with all the laundry. That was Ammiji and Farhana's job. Then Ammiji sent Dad and Faraz out to the market with a long list and strict instructions to come straight home.

Several hours later, the newly scrubbed kitchen cupboards groaned under the weight of family-sized tins of ghee, lentils, garam flour, sugar, honey, dates from Madinah, bottles of Zamzam water that a neighbour had brought from Makkah, fruit juice, mango powder, new packets of turmeric, chilli, coriander, cumin and Ammiji's homemade chaat and garam masala.

How ironic, thought Farhana, as she watched her father and brother drag in the bags of shopping, *it's meant to be a month of fasting but we think about food more than ever.*

Later that day, when Ammiji and Dad had gone out to take some shopping over to his mum's, Naneeji's, house to save her a trip out in the rain, their father's youngest sister, Auntie Najma, came over.

Faraz raced to the door when he heard the bell from up in his room. Auntie Najma stood on the doorstep, a vision in black in the pouring rain. Her umbrella kept the rain off but it couldn't stop her *jilbab*, her long black cloak, soaking up the water from the garden path. Her face was covered with a *niqab*, a face veil, her hands with black gloves.

No one seeing Auntie Najma on the street would have any clue that she preferred to wear her *kurta* tunics with faded blue jeans, or that she had a tiny diamond nose ring and a weakness for gourmet sandwiches and designer handbags. A few words exchanged in a shop or on the bus would not betray her First Class degree or love of world literature and Impressionist art. To passers-by, she was just another woman in *purdah*, a common enough sight in their part of town, an unwelcome oddity in the town centre and the suburbs.

But Faraz and Farhana had long since ceased to be surprised by their aunt's outward appearance, even though the whole family had been shocked by how changed she had been when she had come back from university in London. Auntie Najma, once so wild and out of control, had come back all Islamic. The change had been a real shock.

"I can't stand it when people take things to extremes…" Ammiji would often say. But extreme or not, Auntie Najma was by far the twins' favourite relative and, as far as they were concerned, she was welcome any time.

"Faraz!" Auntie Najma said warmly. "*Asalaamu alaikum*! Where've you been, man? I thought you were going to come and see us last weekend." Her gravelly voice was unmistakable.

"*Wa alaikum salaam*, Auntie," Faraz replied, his face breaking into a smile. He opened the door and stepped aside for her to walk past him into the hallway. "Dad wanted me to help him in the shop, y'know?"

Once inside, Auntie Najma flipped up her *niqab* and gave him another big smile, pulling off her gloves. "How are you, love?"

"Fine, Auntie, I'm good."

"*Alhamdulillah*, that's great…"

"Auntie Naj!" Farhana had heard her aunt's voice from upstairs and ran down to greet her.

The two of them hugged and Auntie Najma laughed. "All right, all right, easy!" Then she turned to Faraz. "Are you two free for a couple of hours? I wanted you to come and help me with a few Ramadan preparations…"

The twins looked at each other.

"I guess so," said Farhana. "Ammiji and Dad have gone to Naneeji's with some groceries."

"Well, just call and find out if it's OK, in case there's something else she wants you to do at home… I know what the weekend before Ramadan can be like!"

Farhana ran off to the living room to call her mother.

Faraz started putting on his trainers, hunting for his jacket. "Faraz," said Auntie Najma, "have you got any jackets you don't wear any more?"

"Ummm, I don't think so…"

"What about that one there?" Auntie Najma pointed to a jacket with a red hood. "I remember you wearing that last year – there's no way you can fit into it now!"

Faraz smiled and blushed. He had grown *a lot* since last year. After a few minutes, he had unearthed several coats and jackets that he had outgrown.

"What d'you need them for anyway, Auntie?" he asked as he pushed them into a big shopping bag.

"Well, the weather's starting to change, and there are quite a few people who would be glad of a Faraz Ahmed cast-off."

By the time they left the house, they had three carrier bags full of warm clothes and shoes. Auntie Najma packed them in the boot of her little Mini.

Farhana smiled at the sight: this woman in black, covered from head to foot, at the wheel of a bright red Mini Cooper. What did the neighbours make of *that*?

The three of them chatted easily as they drove slowly along the rainy Saturday high street.

Outside the car windows, it was as if the sights, sounds and smells of downtown Karachi had followed the immigrants who had come over in the fifties and had clung on, in spite of the concrete buildings and English weather.

The damp streets were packed with shoppers picking up supplies for the weeks ahead. Beards, skull caps, headscarves, *dupattas, burqas, shalwar kamees*, mixed and mingled and created a vivid roadside display. *Saris* and *shalwar kameez* vied for window space, a competition between the traditional styles and the latest Asian designer looks. Impossibly bright gold jewellery glittered in the jewellery shop windows, fake versions adorning shoes, evening bags and shop mannequins. The fruit'n'veg stalls boasted their finest South Asian vegetables – *mooli, karela,* okra, red chillies – and fruit by the box or the kilo: plump, fragrant mangoes, hairy coconuts, *sapodilla*.

In other shops, darkened places whose spicy, dusty odour tickled the nose, there were sacks of rice, grains, lentils and dried coriander, tubs of ground cumin, golden turmeric, and cardamom pods. The halal butchers had people queuing up outside and, all the while, the delivery vans kept coming.

Practically everyone here was Asian. Once in a while, you might see an old white man or woman, walking a dog or pulling a trolley, but they were a rarity, like relics from a bygone age. This was the closest you could get to Pakistan without a plane ticket.

But Auntie Najma didn't stop. They carried on driving until they'd left their neighbourhood behind them and were heading towards the other side of town.

"Where are we going, Auntie?" Farhana asked at last.

"Well," Auntie Najma replied, "I've started volunteering at a women's homeless shelter twice a week, and I promised someone I would be there today."

The twins looked at each other. Homeless shelter? Auntie Najma caught their shared look and smiled.

"Relax!" she said. "I'm not going to make you wash all the dishes in the soup kitchen or anything! I won't be long at all. You guys don't even have to come out – although you can if you like... and, who knows, you might benefit from it...."

After parking the car, Auntie Najma asked the twins to help her with the bags. As it was a women's shelter, Faraz took the bags as far as the door, then waited outside. Auntie Najma signed in, then went to the common room.

Farhana looked around warily, not wanting to stare, but curious about this place and its inhabitants. Some of the women looked at her suspiciously, others stared past her, uninterested.

Auntie Najma, *niqab* up, walked towards a young lady with more piercings than Farhana could count. Through the fuzz of shaved hair that was growing back, she could see a large tattoo on the woman's scalp. Farhana shivered involuntarily and was about to go when her aunt, all smiles, called her over.

"Alice," she said, "I'd like you to meet my niece, Farhana... Farhana, this is Alice."

Farhana tried to smile and sound normal. "Hi..."

"Hi," said Alice in a soft voice that didn't seem to match her appearance. "So you're the special niece I've heard so much about!"

Farhana looked questioningly over at Auntie

Najma who grinned. "You know I'm always showing off to everyone about my bright, beautiful, wonderful niece, *masha Allah*!"

Farhana smiled, embarrassed. "Well," she said at last, "it was nice meeting you…" She didn't know what else to say. But it was clear that Auntie Najma and Alice did not have a shortage of things to say to each other. They spoke animatedly for about twenty minutes, bursting out laughing several times. Then, Auntie Najma took out some papers and gave them to Alice, who smiled gratefully.

"Thanks so much, Najma," Farhana heard her say. "I don't know what I would do without you."

"Don't mention it," was Auntie Najma's response. "We'll see that justice is served, *insha Allah*."

Alice smiled then, showing two gaps where her teeth were missing. "Yeah, *insha Allah*…"

The two women embraced briefly, then Auntie Najma flew back to Farhana.

"Is that lady Muslim?" Farhana wanted to know.

"No," smiled Auntie Najma, "she picked up *insha Allah* from me. But you never know…."

* * *

Soon they were all sitting in a booth on retro red leather benches, studying a menu made up entirely of milkshakes.

"Hmmm," murmured Auntie Najma, "I *still* haven't tried every flavour. But I think it's banana peanut butter for me. What will you two have?"

The twins stared at the menu, overwhelmed by the choice.

Auntie Najma smiled at them. "Take your time, it's OK..." She pulled a brocade-covered book out of her Moroccan leather bag.

"What's that, Auntie Naj?" asked Farhana, peering over at it.

"It's my journal," answered her aunt, flipping the pages. "Ramadan is in a few days' time, isn't it? So, I'm using my journal to prepare for Ramadan, to make sure I have a list of things that I want to achieve, stuff I want to improve on, things I want to do...."

Farhana raised her eyebrows. Auntie Naj still had stuff to improve on? "Like what?"

"Ummm," Auntie Najma's eyes scanned the page. "Like finish reading the *Qur'an*, pray the night prayer, give some of my clothes to charity, take my favourite niece and nephew to *iftar* at a new restaurant that's opened up... that kind of thing." She looked up at them and grinned. "So, how do *you* prepare for Ramadan?"

Faraz and Farhana looked at each other and then at their aunt, puzzled.

"What do you mean, Auntie?" asked Faraz. "What's to prepare? OK, I'm ready to go hungry, if that's what you mean..."

"Unlike last year, y'mean?" Farhana couldn't resist having a dig at her brother's pathetic show of fasting the year before.

Faraz gave her a dirty look. "Yeah, unlike last year! And don't start with me! I know about you and Shazia down the chip shop!"

Farhana blushed. "That was different!" she protested hotly. "Shazia wasn't praying at the time! And anyway, I ... I..."

Faraz burst out laughing. "Save it for the judge, mate! You were just as rubbish as me, admit it!"

Farhana giggled sheepishly.

"Well, none of that this year you two, all right?" Their aunt looked at them sternly, only the slightest hint of a smile about her lips.

Then the waiter was there to take their order. Farhana thought she would be adventurous and try the Blackberry Cheesecake Shake. Faraz decided to play it safe with a strawberry vanilla blend.

"It's those strawberry protein shakes, Faraz!" joked Farhana. "They've ruined your taste buds for life!"

The twins laughed. It had been a while since they had been out together: just the two of them and Auntie Naj.

"OK, let's take a few steps back here," said Auntie Najma. "I want you to tell me about Ramadan. What it's all about, what it's for."

The twins looked at each other and rolled their eyes – *what was this, madressah?* Then they shrugged their shoulders and rattled off everything they knew about Ramadan, the month of mercy: no food or drink from sunrise to sunset, one of the pillars of Islam, devils chained up, time to do good deeds, forgiveness for the one who fasts the whole month.

"OK, good, so you know the basics," said Auntie Najma. "I expect you're well pleased with yourselves! But what does Ramadan mean to *you*? What do *you* want to get out of it?"

The two fell silent. They weren't used to being asked about their own views on religious matters.

As a young Muslim, you did what you were supposed to do, what your parents told you, no questions.

"Auntie," said Faraz at last, "Ramzan is just something that you do: everyone does. It's about family and food, big *iftars* and going mosque on Eid. It's just the norm."

"But what I mean is, what do *you* want to achieve by the end of Ramadan? What do you hope to gain?"

They were silent for a moment. Farhana spoke up first.

"I guess I'd like to prove to myself that I can actually fast the whole month... I've never done the whole month before."

Faraz nodded in agreement. "I suppose it's a challenge, really. Cos it's hard, innit? The question is: can you handle it?"

"And it's not just the fasting, is it?" added Farhana. "It's the other stuff, the stuff you know you shouldn't be doing in the first place... messing about."

"Trying to better yourself, as a person, as a Muslim."

"Trying to live up to your ideals..."

Auntie Najma smiled at them both. "Now that's what *I'm* talking about! We have to remember how fortunate we are to see another Ramadan. It's like we've been given another chance to repent, to better ourselves, to get some serious blessings from Allah. We've got a chance to make this month really special... I can't wait!" She fished around in her bag. "Look, here's a book I've been reading, just to remind myself, y'know?"

She showed them the book: *Ramadan in the Qur'an and Sunnah*.

Farhana's eyes lit up, as they always did when she saw a book she hadn't read.

"D'you think I could borrow that, Auntie?"

"Of course – but only if you let Faraz have a read too..."

"You'd better let me have it first, Auntie, or I'll never get a look-in once it disappears into Farhana's room!"

They all laughed and Auntie Najma handed him the book. Then the milkshakes came and there was no time for talk. None of them remembered that they hadn't even eaten lunch!

★ ★ ★

Faraz looked down again at the line in the book that lay open on his lap:

'*Fasting has been prescribed for you so that you may attain righteousness...*'

Could he possibly attain that? Reach that point of awareness? Stay out of the madness? He wanted to try, wanted to so badly. He would make a go of it this year, he really would.

But a little voice in the back of his mind whispered treacherous thoughts: *What about Skrooz? And the lads? What will they think?*

He pushed that thought aside. In this place, at this moment, there was nothing he wanted more than to attain righteousness, to feel at peace with himself.

He took a deep breath.

He would do it, *insha Allah*, he would. He just had to stay focused.

★ ★ ★

That night, Farhana stayed up after everyone else had gone to bed. She sat up in bed, her duvet pulled up over her knees, an open book on her lap, writing by lamplight. She was making a list.

All evening, she had been thinking about what her aunt had said and, all evening, she had asked herself questions: *what do you want? Where are you going? How can you improve?*

Now she had written the answers on a page in the open book. As she wrote them, they became real somehow, concrete, as if they took life from the page they now covered.

Pray on time
Read more Qur'an
Stop gossiping
Give away some stuff
Help the needy
Study hard
Get coursework done ahead of schedule
Pray the night prayer

Her eyes flickered upwards to the white *hijab* once again. Her hand hesitated as she formulated the sentence in her head:

Start wearing hijab.

Could she really do it?

She knew one thing for sure: if she put it on, she wanted to do it properly, for good, not taking it off again after a few weeks, or after Eid. She didn't want to be a hypocrite. But was she ready to be a '*hijabi*'? In the fullest sense of the word? After all, *hijab* wasn't just about covering your hair. It was about a state of mind: modesty, awareness of God, awareness of your actions, being accountable, being a walking symbol of Islam.

After many discussions with Auntie Najma, and debates with her mum and her mate Shazia, who wore the *hijab*, albeit reluctantly, she now believed that the *hijab* was a religious obligation, an act of worship that would be rewarded.

That wasn't the issue.

The issue was whether or not she could live up to its expectations – and whether she could deal with the negative reactions she was sure to encounter at school.

'*And I did not create mankind or the jinn except to worship Me.*'

If that was her reason for living, what was stopping her from taking this step?

Why should I care what the girls at school think? she thought. *Or my teachers? After school, they go back to their lives, to their kids. They're not living their lives thinking about me.*

Farhana turned the various discussions over in her mind again and again, arguing with herself. One person's name kept coming up again and again – Malik – but she consciously pushed it aside. She was not about to let his ideas or opinions influence her, not now.

By the time she turned out the light, she was mentally exhausted but pleased with the outcome of her internal dialogue.

I'm going to try. If this is the right thing, Allah will make it easy for me. I'll just have to trust Him on this one.

Then, just before turning out the light, she scribbled one last thing:

GOM

Get over Malik.

* * *

Across the hallway, in his room, Faraz was praying *Isha*, the last prayer of the day. It was the prayer he prayed most frequently as it could be offered just before bed, no waking early in the morning, no missing lunch.

O Allah, Ramzan is on its way.
Got to get meself sorted.
No more wasting time.
No more messing about.
Just me and You.
One on one.

It's not easy being me, being Faraz. At school they think I'm a loser, thick. But that's not what Skrooz says. 'Fraz the Wrecker'. That's his name for me. He says I've got it in me to be someone, to prove meself.

But not this month. Not yet. This month, I want to be a good Muslim, a good boy, a nice Pakistani boy who goes mosque, prays on time, stays out of trouble.

Yeah, I figure I can be good for one month. Insha Allah.

It should be easy to put Skrooz off for a few weeks, just until after Eid. He didn't want that side of his life messing with his Ramadan – this month was sacred.

Chapter 3

A taste of trouble

On Monday morning, brother and sister walked together to the bus stop. When they were younger, they had been inseparable, often not needing to speak when together. It was as if they knew instinctively what the other was thinking and feeling. But times had changed. The move to high school and adolescence had put an end to that effortless understanding. Now when they were silent, it was just as likely that they were both lost in their own thoughts, totally unaware of each other's secrets.

But hanging out with Auntie Naj had started to bring them closer again. They had slowly begun to open up.

Farhana spoke first. "You looking forward to Ramadan, then?"

Faraz nodded. "I reckon I'm gonna make a go of it this year, sis."

"Yeah, me too," Farhana answered. "That conversation we had with Auntie Najma over the weekend really got me thinking about Ramzan, and what it really means…"

"You mean like it not being just about going hungry? About it being a chance to make a change for the better?"

"Yeah, that's right," Farhana smiled at her brother. She had seen his face, so similar to hers, light up as her aunt had described the blessings of Ramadan. 'The month of mercy' she had called it, when all your sins could be forgiven, when Allah Himself would reward your sacrifice.

"I could do with turning over a new leaf in some areas, you know," she said meaningfully.

"So, what about Malik, then?" Faraz only had sketchy details about Farhana's involvement with Malik but he knew enough. . . .

"Don't go there, Faraz," mumbled his sister, looking away. "There's nothing there now…" Then she turned back to him. "What about you? What about Skrooz and the lads?"

"I reckon I can keep them off my back…"

"Yeah, I think that's best. I don't know about you hanging with lads like that anyway. Plus this is not the year to be messing about, not with exams around the corner." She said that even though she knew that exams were the furthest thing from Faraz's mind. They just weren't on his radar.

"Exams? Ah, yeah, that's right... no problem."

Farhana looked at him, a touch of sadness in her eyes. "You'd ace them if you studied, Faraz, you know that."

"Yeah, yeah, we all know that you got the brains between us!" Faraz had heard that comment too many times from family members. It still stung.

"That's absolute rubbish, Faraz, and you know it!" Farhana snapped. "You just need to try harder, that's all..."

"All right, all right! No lectures today, yeah? You made your point!" He ducked as Farhana swung her schoolbag at his head.

"You two at it again, are you?" They both swung round to see Farhana's friend, Shazia, standing behind them, an amused look on her face.

"Hey, Shazia!" Farhana hugged her friend. "*Asalaamu alaikum*, you're late."

35

"*Wa alaikum salaam*," Shazia replied briefly. "Yeah, didn't get much sleep last night – was helping Mum with some stuff."

Faraz stood awkwardly to the side, trying not to stare at Shazia, *Imam* Shakir's daughter, his sister's best friend since forever, the girl of his dreams. But he was aware of her presence, of the smell of her hair, neatly tucked under a white *hijab*.

He had to greet her properly though, to be polite. "*Asalaamu alaikum*, Shazia," he mumbled, sweat springing up under his collar.

"*Wa alaikum salaam*, Faraz," Shazia answered, glancing at him.

Then they all heard a great roar, a revving and squeal of tyres, a great rush of horsepower far too loud and powerful for their quiet road. They turned to look.

A black BMW, low and shiny, was speeding down their narrow street. Loud hip- hop blared out of the windows and the bass made the pavement throb.

Farhana and Shazia both winced at the swear words that bounced off windows decorated with the word *bismillah*, in the name of Allah. The car sped towards them, tearing up the tarmac until it came to a screeching halt in front of them.

What a motor! thought Faraz, admiring the car's sleek lines and impressive alloy wheels, almost in spite of himself. He had never had the usual lads' interests – but this car, its raw power and energy, stirred something inside him.

Then the tinted window on the passenger side slid down and an Asian boy with a spiky Mohawk and silver knuckle dusters on his fingers leaned out.

"Fraz!" he called. "What's goin' on, bruv?"

Shazia looked over at Farhana. Faraz knew these guys?

The driver's door opened and another Asian guy stepped out of the car. He was a monster, this one. A huge hunk of towering flesh and muscle, scarred and tattooed, squeezed into tight jeans and a hoody. Thick silver chains adorned his chest, diamond rings on his sausage-like fingers. His dark hair was cut so short that the skin of his scalp shone through.

Immediately, Farhana knew who it was. It was Skrooz.

"Hey, bruv," he called over to Faraz, who

hurried towards him and pumped his hand. Skrooz drew him close in an embrace, his great arm across Faraz's back, his cigarette smouldering between his fat fingers, his eyes on Farhana.

Farhana felt her skin crawl as his eyes raked up and down her body, his lips twisted in a half smile. He winked at her and she turned away, feeling exposed and vulnerable.

Then he turned to Faraz.

"Where you been, blud?" he asked. "You want a lift to school? I'm droppin' my little brother off…"

"Y-you mean that?" Faraz's eyes were wide.

"Yeah, why not?" He opened the back door and Faraz practically leapt in, hardly looking back. He ran his hand over the leather seats as they vibrated to the music beneath his fingers. *Cool.*

Skrooz turned to Farhana and Shazia.

"So, you ladies want a lift too?" He smiled again before taking another drag of his cigarette.

"Er, no, that's OK," stuttered Farhana. "Our bus is here. Thanks." And with that, she pulled Shazia towards the waiting bus.

They heard the car start up again and, with the

squeal of burning rubber, it lurched into the road and roared away.

Neither girl spoke.

Then Shazia turned to Farhana and said, "Your brother's heading for trouble, he is."

Chapter 4

An invitation

Farhana loved her school. Her parents had decided to send her to the local girls' school, rather than the mixed comprehensive Faraz went to – and Farhana couldn't have been happier. Of course, her parents' motives had been almost solely to keep her 'out of trouble', ie away from boys but, as it happened, Middleton School was actually an excellent school and the mixture of challenges and incentives really suited Farhana. It was left for Faraz to deal with the gangs and exhausted teachers at his inner city comprehensive.

What with a full programme of lessons, basketball, debate club, lunchtime gossip and ever-shifting loyalties, Farhana was in her element. Somehow, with her good looks and easy charm, she had always found herself riding the crest of the wave of popular opinion: she was liked and admired by almost everyone. And her teachers adored her. Ever since the first year, they had told her that she was bright, that with hard work and focus she would excel and make them proud. "If all that Bollywood stuff doesn't go to your head!"

And Farhana found learning easy. Her mind soaked up information, facts, opinions, calculations, graphs, theories. It turned them all over, studying them carefully before storing them away to be used in a class discussion, in a debate or in an essay that would earn top marks.

Her parents knew this about her and were mildly proud. What was it Ammiji had said? 'Farhana is a clever girl, *masha Allah*. She and Sajid are so well matched!'

When she thought of her cousin Sajid, the medical student from Karachi, the 'nice, polite boy', her heart twisted, sometimes with curiosity, other times with rebellion. *What if I don't want a 'nice, polite boy'?*

But those were battles for another time, for later. She knew about her parents' hopes for her and Sajid and she was careful never to mention the idea of marriage, in case they decided to press the issue. The last thing she wanted was her aunties on her case.

It was funny that, her mild schizophrenia. From her observations, it was a condition that practically all the Asian girls she knew suffered from. It was about having one persona at school, with your friends and with non-Asians, and a completely different persona at home. At school, she was intelligent, a bit cheeky, chatty and outgoing.

But home was another story. There, she was completely different. She was quieter, for a start, less likely to offer an opinion, certainly not one to argue. She did as she was told and listened to adults' conversations respectfully, never butting in, never challenging their views, even when she had reason to.

It was as if the two Farhanas were completely different. Her teachers would not recognise their favourite feisty student in the dutiful daughter she was at home. And her parents would most probably have been appalled to see their well-brought-up daughter arguing with the teachers, teasing her friends, being crowned queen of the Bollywood Massive.

But what did she expect? Her outside world was different to theirs. Her mother, born and raised in Pakistan, had never cried while reading *Of Mice and Men*. Her father, having left school at sixteen to work for his dad in his restaurant, had long forgotten about the causes of the Second World War. Neither of them could explain the theory of relativity or list five sources of renewable energy. All that had nothing to do with them and their world, which revolved around the family and their newsagent's shop.

The learning, the facts and figures, were Farhana's alone, to ponder over in her bedroom at the desk that her mother tidied scrupulously each day. Sometimes, Faraz would take an interest but, for the most part, they were her private pleasure. Which was a good thing, considering that it was her GCSE year. And her teachers had predicted mostly 'A's for her GCSEs – all except Art. She was rubbish at Art, unlike Faraz who, in her opinion, was a particularly gifted artist. If only he would pursue it....

"So, Farhana," Auntie Najma had asked once day, "what do you want to be when you grow up?"

Farhana had laughed. "Honestly?"

Her aunt had nodded.

Farhana had faced her and said, "I'm going to do my 'A' Levels and apply for university, somewhere far away from here, out in the wide, wide world…" She looked at her aunt steadily, almost daring her to say it couldn't be done, that she was reaching too far, that her parents would never allow it.

But her aunt just smiled and whispered, "Like I did?"

Farhana nodded emphatically. "Like you did."

She had never shared these thoughts with her parents, knowing that they would much prefer her to take a Childcare course at the local college and get a job in a school, at least until it was time to get married. But with Auntie Naj, she was never afraid to dream big dreams.

But for now, there was no talk of marriage – just books and study and trips to the town centre, secret text messages and a little flirting – nothing serious.

Until Malik.

"Would your parents ever let you bring someone home?" she had once asked Shazia.

"Are you crazy?" Shazia had screeched, her eyes almost popping out of her head. "Of course not!

My dad would lock me up if he suspected I even *knew* any guys, let alone talked to them! And bring one home? That is totally out of the question!"

"I don't see why Asian parents have to be so controlling," their friend Robina had opined. "I mean, why can't they let their kids make their own decisions? What's it got to do with them? Look at my friend, Katie, her mum is so cool! She can bring guys home, no problem. Her mum even lets them sleep over."

Shazia's eyes grew wider still. "What? That's mad, that is!"

But Robina shrugged her slim shoulders. "She says it's better that Katie bring them home where she can keep an eye on them, where she can make sure she's safe, than she go sneaking around with boys her mum doesn't know. A very enlightened attitude, if you ask me."

"Yeah, but Katie's not *desi*, Asian, is she?" Farhana put in. "We're not even supposed to be talking to boys, let alone sneaking around with them, remember?"

Robina rolled her eyes. "Oh, give me a break! That is so naïve! Tons of Asian girls are doing it and keeping it a secret from their parents –

you just ask my sister! And why not? Why should the goris – *and* Asian guys! - have all the fun? Why shouldn't we let our hair down and enjoy ourselves – at least before we are chained to the kitchen sink and flipping *roti* for an overweight husband sitting in front of the telly!"

They had all laughed at that. But Robina's strident anti-tradition rhetoric had bothered Farhana. Did she want to live like Katie and her mum? They shopped together for the same skinny jeans and halter-neck tops, went out clubbing together and fancied the same guys.

She thought of her own mother, all modest *shalwar kameez* and respect for tradition, always home when she got home from school, a constant, steadying presence. No, she didn't want to swap....

★ ★ ★

"So, are you guys coming to the Asian Girl Bachelor Party next weekend?" As they walked down the stairs towards their next lesson, Robina turned to Shazia and Farhana and showed them a flyer. A bikini-clad woman with dark eyes and endless legs was draped over a brooding Asian man with designer stubble and a diamond earring.

Shazia wrinkled up her nose in disgust. "That is too disgusting! What a cheap flyer!"

But Robina turned and flicked her with the glossy piece of card.

"It's not for the likes of you, Shazia!" she laughed. "I think it's going to be dead classy – and I bet my sister can get us tickets. All the staff at Asian Girl will be getting free passes."

Farhana remembered how they had pored over the bachelor issue of Asian Girl for ages in her room, deciding which of the guys were hot, which were right posers and which ones were wearing too much make-up. Her brother Faraz had caught them at it and wouldn't stop teasing her about it. In the end, she had had to put it in the recycling bin to hide it from her mum and dad.

"So when is it then?" Farhana asked. *As if I'll be going*, she thought to herself.

Robina looked at the flyer again. "It says next Saturday night here."

"But we'll be fasting then. Ramzan is in a few days' time y'know…" Farhana took out her mobile to check her messages. Several times, she pressed the button to delete. Five messages from him so far today.

"So? At least it's the weekend, right?"

"Oh, don't be so daft, Robina!" snapped Shazia. "Are you really going clubbing during Ramzan?"

Robina shrugged her shoulders. "Well, I'm sixteen now – my parents can't tell me nothing. And besides, if I go with my sister, it should be all right…"

Farhana and Shazia looked at each other. Robina had changed so much since she started hanging with her older sister, Tasnim, who had a glamorous job at a hip Asian magazine and lived it up every weekend. Once upon a time, they had all been on the same page, but now…

"Well, I won't be going," said Farhana at last. "I know how busy things always are in Ramadan – besides I want to do it right this year and …"

"Yeah, yeah, whatever!" Robina huffed. "I'll let you know how fun it was, OK? Take a few pics on my phone for you."

"Don't bother," muttered Shazia, not quite under her breath.

Robina took a long, hard look at Shazia. "You know what, Shazia?" Her voice was slow and deliberate. "You really need to get a life."

And with that, she turned on her heel and flounced off down the hall.

The two girls watched her go.

"She's got some serious issues, man," said Shazia, as they too began to walk to their next class: Art.

Chapter 5

Masterpiece

Faraz sat hunched over the large sheet of grainy paper.

All around him, the sounds of the unruly Year 11s ebbed and flowed: papers shuffling, chairs scraping, doors slamming, whispered arguments, sly curses and promises to meet after school, either for a tryst or a fight. He was hardly aware of his hard chair and the scarred desk, etched with messages from students long gone. In the background, he could hear the soft voice of Mr McCarthy, the art teacher, trying to maintain order and command respect in a class of hard-boiled teens, all eager to protest, argue, trip him up.

But Faraz was hardly conscious of the chaos. His mind was focused. He was in the zone. This was where he felt safe, where he could do something right...

"No, Faraz, no! That's wrong! Do it again!"
Imam Shakir's voice echoed in his subconscious
and he heard again the titters of the other kids,
all careful not to laugh out loud in case the *imam*
called on them next. Or turned the stick on them.

Faraz, six years old, took a deep breath.

"B-b-b-b-bismillahir-r-r-r-r-rahmanir-r-r-r-
r-r-raheem-m-m," he stammered, tears stinging
his eyes.

Imam Shakir shook his head in frustration.
"You don't practise, Faraz! You lazy boy!" He picked
up the little stick he kept on the bench at the front
of the room. "Put your hand out!"

Faraz swallowed hard as the *imam* made his
way towards him through the rows of children.
The room swam before him: the pea green walls,
the single strip of neon light, the blackboard
with undecipherable Arabic and Urdu letters,
the benches stacked along the sides of the rooms,
his sister Farhana's face, miserable, ashamed for
him, the carpet beneath his feet green, the colour
of Jannah, Paradise.

Then the *imam* was in front of him, a resigned

look on his face, his stick raised. Faraz's fingers trembled but he dared not pull them away, knowing he would get an extra beating.

The stick whistled through the air and landed with a thwack on his upturned palm and fingers. Heat seared his skin, more tears, dropping down his face this time, adding to his shame.

The other children were subdued now, feeling his pain. They had all felt the *imam*'s stick at one time or another.

"Practise your *surahs*, you lazy boy!" the *imam* shouted, furious at having to interrupt his lesson to deal with the boy again. He would just have to work harder at controlling his tongue, that was all. He would speak to his father after Friday prayers.

Faraz knew what it felt like not to belong. He had never made much progress with *Imam* Shakir at *madressah* and had dropped out as soon as he was allowed to. He had tried to fulfil his father's sporting dreams by being the cricketer his father had been but he couldn't bat or bowl to save his life. He had tried with football but with two left feet, football stardom was not an option. He had tried hard to fit in at school but he had always been too shy, too sensitive, too pretty for the other boys who had made it their mission in life to mess up his face as best they could.

But in the art room, he didn't need to try and fit in – he belonged there. He understood how colours worked, how to coax feeling out of a lump of clay, how to make a paintbrush sing. This was his sanctuary.

Now, with quick, nimble movements his fingers attacked the page, stabbing, stroking, the charcoal dust rising off the paper, staining his fingers. He worked intently, furiously, adding lines, contours, shades, cross hatching, blending, the image growing all the time, until it filled the page.

The assignment was one of his favourites: Imaginative Composition. Mr McCarthy had asked them to draw an imaginary landscape, a long shot for kids who had scarcely seen more than the inside of their estate and the town centre.

Faraz had chosen his favourite medium – charcoal – and, while his classmates stalled and argued, hoping for the bell to ring, he poured himself onto the page.

It was a landscape he had seen in a dream the night before.

He was running, running in the dark. Something

was after him, something he couldn't see, couldn't hear. But he could feel it, gaining on him. The street lights swam and made mad patterns before his eyes as he raced by. The skyline was unfamiliar: what looked like the domes of mosques loomed high, jostling with high rise flats, pointed spires and spiky fence-tops, weird shapes from another time, from another world. The road began to slope upwards, up, up, steeper and steeper until he was climbing it like the side of a mountain, scrabbling for a foothold, a crack in the road, anything to keep himself from sliding backwards, backwards into darkness...

The dream had been quite vivid and he was feverish with excitement as he watched his dreamscape come to life on the page. Everything around him blurred as he sketched, panting slightly, fearing the sound of the bell at any minute.

It was only when he felt himself coming to the end, seeing what he had seen in his mind's eye, that he became aware of the small crowd that had gathered round him.

Then it was finished.

He leaned back in his chair, let out a long ragged breath and threw his tiny piece of charcoal down, wiping the sweat from his forehead, leaving a dark smudge along his hairline.

His classmates stood by, riveted, studying the skyline, the strange silhouettes, the masterful strokes, the sense of strangeness, darkness and dread as the night sky loomed above an alien city.

A few of them whispered and Mr McCarthy nodded approvingly. *This lad will go far if he keeps straight.*

Faraz was his brightest student, although other staff members often complained about his attitude, his laziness, his wasted potential. They were all sure he was going to fail his GCSEs. But not here, in the Art Room. This was where he came alive.

But the moment was broken by Maj, a broad slab of muscle with a permanent smirk. "What have you got there, Faraz?" he taunted as he pushed his way to the front of the crowd.

Faraz forced himself to look him in the eye, although his heart missed a beat when he remembered their last encounter after school. His mum had fussed for ages over his cut lip and bruised face. 'Just some kids at school, Ammiji, don't worry. I can handle it.'

He hadn't told her that it was Maj, who belonged to a gang that was forever sparring with Skrooz and his crew. And now, he was involved too. An enemy of the lads was his enemy too, after all.

He narrowed his eyes, ready for a confrontation.

"Ooohh," minced Maj, striking an effeminate pose. "So Faraz is an ahhhhtist, eh?"

Some of the others tittered and Mr McCarthy coughed and adjusted his heavy glasses, ready to intervene.

But Maj didn't give him the chance. "It's a pity charcoal can be rubbed out," he said and, with a slow, deliberate motion, he swept his hand across the painting. The domes, tower blocks and spikes merged into the night sky in a black rainbow arc. "Just like that."

A tremor ran through the class. Several girls gasped and Mr McCarthy covered his mouth, powerless in the face of the tension, the restless adolescent energy that could so easily spill blood. He cleared his throat, ready to reassert his authority, bracing himself.

Faraz stared at his creation, now ruined beyond repair and he felt the pressure build up behind his eyes, heat flooding his brain.

Abruptly, he pushed his chair back and it

toppled over, scattering the boys and girls behind him.

"Maj, what's wrong with you, man? What you trying to prove?"

Maj sneered, looking Faraz up and down. "That you're nothing, mate. You always have been and you always will be, no matter who you hang with – Skrooz can't help you here."

Faraz thought of all the years of anonymity, of blending into the shadows, of keeping his head down. How the other kids had teased him about his stutter, his parents' little newsagent shop, his beautiful green eyes and the fact that he couldn't fight back if the older boys pushed him around.

But that was then. He was older now, bigger, tougher. He wouldn't stand for that kind of disrespect any more, not now that he was part of Skrooz's crew.

He looked at Maj and considered jumping him, but one look at his beefy arms straining against his school shirt made him think again. Not here, not now. He couldn't win this round.

"Yeah? We'll see about that." And he stared Maj down, steeling his eyes against the fear that constricted his heart.

And then, in the next moment, he grabbed his bag and pushed past everyone as the bell rang, shrill in the crackling silence of the art room.

Chapter 6

Malik

Farhana dashed up the street, her schoolbag over her head, her school skirt soaking wet. A few metres, the creak of a gate, a puddle-filled path and a slippery key and she had her front door open. She stood there, dripping on to the welcome mat, inhaling the smell of frying chillies and garlic, listening to the hiss of hot oil. Ammiji was making *samosas*.

She also heard the sound of other voices, her Auntie Sajda's high-pitched laugh and her grandmother's strident bark - and it dawned on her. Of course! Ramzan was around the corner. It was time to start making *samosas, pakhoras* and *rotis* for the freezer.

Although Ammiji was the daughter-in-law, family and friends liked gathering at their house because they had a big kitchen and the conversation was always as good as the tea.

"*Asalaamu alaikum*, Ammiji!" she called out, knowing that they hadn't heard her come in.

There was a chorus of returned greetings and her mum came out of the kitchen, wiping her floury hands on her apron. Her hair was coming out of her bun and she had a streak of flour on her cheek, but Farhana couldn't help thinking how beautiful she still was, even at the ripe old age of forty four.

"Oh, look at you!" she cried, taking Farhana's bag from her. "You're soaked! You'd better have a warm shower and change your clothes before you come in. Khala Sajda is dying to see you!"

Farhana smiled and nodded, taking off her waterlogged shoes and handing them to her mother.

"I'll be right down, Ammiji," she said.

"*Insha Allah*," was her mother's response.

As Farhana made her way upstairs, her mobile phone rang. She fished it out of her bag and looked at the number. She bit her lip and cut the call, switching the phone off.

Would he ever stop ringing?

She was done with Malik, that was for sure.

It had been a brief few months of madness, a situation she knew would end in tears. But he was only the most gorgeous Asian guy in the boys' school across the park. Who would have been able to resist him?

Malik had typical Bollywood good looks - gorgeous glossy dark hair, eyes the colour of hazelnuts, a strong jaw with a hint of stubble - and a smooth, deep voice that sounded like melted chocolate.

His eyes had met hers at the inter-schools debate competition. Her heart had quickened but she held his gaze only for a moment before looking away. She wasn't about to let him think she was impressed.

It was only later, when the debate was in mid-flow, that he caught her eye again. The debate had been vigorous and Farhana was well prepared: her eloquent, passionate opening speech had floored her opponents. And that was when she saw the look in his eyes: admiration, curiosity and something else she couldn't put her finger on. Again she had looked away haughtily. She had pretended not to know who the girls were talking about on the way home in the bus. He had made quite an impression: good looks and intelligence made such a good package.

Robina had immediately declared that he was hers, and she had pursued him single-mindedly, finding out where he lived, where he hung out, who his mates were, whether he was single, even managing to get hold of his mobile number. But no matter how many times she had tried to orchestrate a meeting and get him to come with her to the many events her sister had free tickets for, Malik seemed only to have eyes for Farhana.

And so it began.

The text messages, the secret calls to her mobile, then the emails, MSN, back and forth, he so determined to get her to agree to a date, she equally determined to keep him at arms' length, like all other guys.

She wasn't stupid. She knew what guys were about, especially guys like him. And she knew that certain things were too precious to gamble, that some things can never be reclaimed once given away. Her mother had taught her well. So she held back, held back, until he wore down her resistance.

His words were too sweet and they drowned out the thought of her parents' shock and complete disapproval. If marriage was not on the cards, there could be no talk of boys. And marriage most certainly was not on the cards at her age. So she couldn't tell Mum about the gifts Malik would give her, little gifts, bought from the department store in town with his hard-earned Saturday wages.

She couldn't tell her about the dreams that left her heart pounding, the blood hot in her veins, her mind deep in a fantasy of happily ever after.

She couldn't tell her how hard it was to concentrate sometimes, how she would hear his voice or see his face while buried deep in an assignment for school.

"The thing is, Shaz," she had confided, "he's not like other boys. We talk, you know? Really talk – about everything! He's interested in me for who I am, not what everyone else sees..."

"That might be true," Shazia insisted, "but I still think there is something wrong with a Muslim boy who starts a relationship with a Muslim girl. I mean, what does he want to get out of it? If he's like all the others and is hoping that he's going to get some of *that*, then he's a ho and I've got zero respect for him! And if he isn't, then why is he doing something he knows we're not allowed to do? What does that say about what he thinks of you?"

"Not everyone is like you, Shazia," Farhana had replied. "Some people know what's right and just find it hard to do it. I don't believe Malik is like all the others... I can't believe that."

"I just don't think I would take the risk – you know what would happen if your parents found out."

"Yeah," Farhana had murmured. "I know..."

And Farhana hadn't told Shazia much about Malik after that. By then, she would have risked anything for Malik. Anything.

Until he did the unthinkable. It was Robina who broke the news. It was she who had seen him at a party with Amba, a tall, leggy girl from the A Level year, the one who was a part-time model for Asian Girl. To hear Robina tell it, Amba didn't seem interested in holding anything back.

And so came the heartache, the pillows wet with tears, the sleepless nights, the gifts thrown in the bin. And she stopped taking his calls, never once telling him why.

Who were you trying to kid? she had asked

herself. *Why should he stay with you when girls ten times prettier than you are fighting to be with him and give him everything he wants and more?*

"More than anything, I'm angry with myself," she had said to Shazia. "I risked so much for him – and for what?"

"Well, I think it's for the best: your parents would have gone absolutely mental if they had found out. I say count your blessings that it ended before things got out of hand. Remember," she had said, putting on her mother's Urdu-tinted accent, "you are their daughter, a Pakistani girl, a Muslim. You are expected to stay chaste, away from all this teen romance nonsense."

Farhana had laughed but she knew that it was true. As far as her parents were concerned, she went to school and came home, clothes deemed too revealing swiftly disappeared, parties were out of the question, staying over at friends' houses was unthinkable.

"We have our way of doing things, Farhana," Mum would say. "It's for your own good."

But how crazy was that? All around her, the messages were the complete opposite. The music, the videos, the movies, the teen magazines were all full of the same thing: boys, boys, boys! It was like, if you weren't hooking up with some guy or the other, you were one of last living freaks.

"I just feel like such an idiot," she had moaned. "You know what Robina said? She said that he had been telling everyone that he was going to 'have' me: Farhana Ahmed, the ice maiden!"

"Yeah, well, I wouldn't take what Robina says too seriously. You know she has a habit of making things up sometimes. Anyway, wasn't she dead set on having Malik herself?"

"Yeah, but she gave up once she saw that he was into me..."

"Yeah?" Shazia had been thoughtful. "OK..."

So Farhana, to protect herself and what was left of her dignity, had closed her heart off, sealing it away. It was all right as long as she didn't hear his voice. So he could call as much as he wanted. There was no way she was going to speak to him.

* * *

When Farhana came downstairs again, she had exchanged her wet school uniform for her favourite *shalwar kameez*, the turquoise one with silver embroidery. Everyone always said that it brought out the colour of her green eyes. Plus she wasn't in the mood for a lecture from her grandmother about the fit of her clothes.

She was greeted in the kitchen by the sight of her mother and aunties all at different stages of the samosa-making process. Ammiji was making the filling – frying the spices, onions and garlic until their smell filled the room, browning the mince.

Auntie Sajda was filling the little squares of filo pastry, folding each one into a neat triangle before putting them in a cloth-covered bowl that was already piled high. Auntie Anisa was overseeing the frying, peering into the deep-fat fryer with a look of intense concentration on her face.

They all turned when she came in, their faces warm with smiles and the heat of the kitchen. Farhana greeted them all in turn, hugging her aunties and kissing her grandmother on the cheek. Then she pulled up a chair and started filling pastry.

"Not like that, Farhana," scolded Auntie Sajda gently. "Watch me. You have to fold the corners, like this, just so."

Farhana did as she was told. She was used

to being bossed around in the kitchen. After all, that was how she had learned to make roti when she was fourteen.

"It's been a long time since I saw Farhana in a *shalwar kameez*, Uzma." Auntie Anisa's voice was teasing as she looked Farhana up and down.

"Well," barked Naneeji, "at least it's better than those terrible skinny jeans she is always wearing!"

They all laughed again and Uzma gave her daughter a hug.

"But you know," Naneeji continued, "the *shalwar kameez* these days are so different to the ones we used to wear, even the ones you girls used to wear. Those *shalwar* were modest, they didn't show your shape. Nowadays, a girl can be wearing *shalwar kameez* and be showing everything at the same time!"

"Ammiji," said Auntie Sajda, looking over at her mother, "you and Babaji used to make us wear *shalwar kameez* at home, even when we didn't want to!"

"And *always* with a *dupatta*!" added Auntie Anisa. "Remember how you used to beat me because I kept losing mine?"

"You were a very careless girl," answered

Naneeji, wagging her finger at her daughter. "And anyway, *shalwar kameez* was our culture, our way. We didn't want you dressing like a *gori*, a white girl. That was OK for school – but not at home. Your father would never have allowed it!"

"Yeah, but look at us now" snorted Auntie Sajda. "As *gori* as they come!"

"Oh, I love to wear *shalwar kameez*!" cried Ammiji. "They are just so elegant and comfortable. I could never have enough of them..."

"Which is great because I get to borrow them!" Farhana piped up. She was used to her aunties and other adults talking about her rather than to her – it was definitely a *desi* thing, an Asian thing. Forty years of living in England hadn't managed to change that. Although sometimes she wished they would listen more and talk less. But just as she was deciding whether to speak up again or not, the doorbell rang.

"Go and get the door, Farhana," ordered Naneeji. "But ask who it is before you open it!"

Farhana smiled ruefully and got up. Her grandmother just could not help playing the matriarch! She looked through the peep hole and immediately yanked the door open.

"Auntie Naj!" she squealed, a huge smile on her face.

"*Asalaamu alaikum*, Farhana-baby!"

Farhana laughed and the two of them embraced on the doorstep.

"Well, let us in then!" laughed Auntie Najma, picking up her long skirts to step into the hallway.

"*Asalaamu alaikum warahmatullahi wabarakatuhu!*" she called out and was answered by a chorus of voices from the kitchen.

Ammiji and Auntie Anisa came out to greet her while Auntie Najma bent down to tug off her sodden boots. Auntie Anisa raised her eyebrows and looked Najma over critically. "I see you dressed for the weather, eh?"

Najma rolled her eyes playfully at her older sister. "Yes, yes, I know, let's put Islam on hold for the awful British weather, shall we?" She stood for a moment, holding her boots.

"Oh, Najma," huffed Ammiji as she took the boots and put them in the airing cupboard. "Why do you always have to take things to extremes?"

But Najma simply smiled at her sister-in-law and held out her arms to embrace her sister.

And all was forgotten.

Auntie Najma took off her *niqab*, *jilbab* and *hijab* and went into the kitchen where she hugged her sisters and gave her mother a kiss and sat down to cut up onions, her usual task as the youngest of four girls.

That's how it is, thought Farhana. *As long as you learn your lines, play your role, you're fine. But just try writing your own script and see what happens.*

"Will you be making *chaat* this year, Sajda?"

"Not sure – I might just buy some; I don't think I can be bothered."

"Tsk, you can be bothered! I will come and make it with you…"

"OK, Ammiji."

"The shop stuff is full of additives anyway, Sajda. Your home-made one is much better."

"Thank you, Najma, you're a sweetie. How is your garden coming along?"

"*Masha Allah*, it's going really well, isn't it, Ammiji? We've been harvesting tomatoes like mad…"

"Oh yes, Farhana brought some home last weekend – they were delicious!"

"Well, they *are* organic, love!"

"Organic? Just fancy words to put the prices up! This is the way we grew things in Pakistan: just the same with no fancy label!"

Farhana giggled. Trust Naneeji to distrust everything!

"I think the *samosas* are all done now... what time are you expecting the others?"

"They said they would come after they feed the kids, about 7:30..."

"*Alhamdulillah*, is Asma coming? I haven't seen her since she had the baby!"

"*Insha Allah*, she'll be coming too – it will be wonderful to see little Umar again."

The women carried on chatting, talking about friends, family, simple things, safe things. It being days before Ramadan, there was no gossip, no 'did you hear?' or 'can you believe?' Farhana felt lulled by their conversation, sleepy almost. It was a nice, secure place to be, amongst family, preparing for Ramadan.

Later that evening, other women came to the house - to join in the Ramadan preparations, to drink tea and to talk. Farhana's dad made it a point to work late, then he went to the mosque with Faraz, knowing that the house would be overrun with women.

The atmosphere in the house was electric: the kitchen steamed with cooking food and hot women's bodies, the conversation was lively, peppered with jokes and Urdu phrases. And, although the English rain poured down outside and the samosa pastry came out of a packet, rather than being made from scratch, the women and their daughters, British-born and raised, felt a sense of history and a connection with the rituals of their foremothers back home in Pakistan. And it felt good.

Chapter 7

Spiritual high

The first night of Ramadan was clear, the sky outside inky black, twinkling with stars. And all across the country and beyond, Muslim households were alive with excitement and anticipation.

They had all heard the news from the mosque: the moon had been sighted, the month of Ramadan had begun. The phone rang constantly with relatives and friends calling to share the good news. The mosque announced that they would pray the *tarawih* prayers that very night, after *isha*, the night prayer, in order to complete the thirty parts of the *Qur'an* before the end of the month.

Faraz got ready to go with his father. He had a shower and wore fresh clothes and a white skull cap, dabbing some perfume oil under his chin.

Farhana had wanted to go too but her mother said they had far too much to do at home.

"But Ammiji," Farhana protested as her father and brother put on their coats, "I want to see what it's like…"

"That's for the men, Farhana," her mum had said crossly. "We have too much to do here."

Faraz threw his sister a pitying look as Farhana scowled. "I don't see why the men get to do all the religious stuff and we get stuck in the kitchen."

Her father frowned, surprised at his normally obedient daughter. "Farhana, that's enough. You go and help your mother. We won't be long."

And, with that, father and son left the house, joining other men from neighbouring houses to walk to their local mosque.

Faraz felt the air buzzing with excitement – the men were jovial, expansive, calling out salaams and 'Ramadan mubarak'. There were quite a few young kids and a few lads around his age, coming along with their dads, most of them wearing white skull caps and long shalwar kameez, their jeans tucked into their trainers.

He recognised some of them from his madressah days, a few others from his school. Their faces were fresh, their clothes just like their fathers'.

These ones aren't on the streets yet – you can tell,
Faraz thought.

They acknowledged each other with brief
nods, a far cry from the handshakes and hugs of
the older generation.

As the mosque filled up, they began to file into
rows behind the *imam*. Faraz followed his father
towards the front of the building and they found
a place right next to a pillar. They had just sat
down when they heard a voice calling out behind
them. They both turned.

A tall young man with a full beard and
shoulder-length wavy hair was making his way
towards them. Faraz had never seen him before
but immediately his eye was drawn to the sketchy
Islamic geometric pattern on the front of his
loose-fitting t-shirt. Sort of reminded him of
classical Arabic calligraphy and graffiti at the same
time.

Dad's face broke into a smile. "Ahh, Imran!
Asalaamu alaikum!" He immediately rose and held
out his hand to the newcomer.

The young man grasped it firmly and shook it,
his other hand on Faraz's dad's arm. "*Wa alaikum
salaam*, uncle, so good to see you." Then he looked

over at Faraz and his eyes lit up. "Is this your son, uncle?"

Faraz nodded and held out his hand, mumbling his greeting.

"*Wa alaikum salaam*, bro, how're you doing?"

"I'm good," was Faraz's reply.

"*Alhamdulillah*," smiled Imran.

Dad turned to Faraz. "Faraz, this is Imran. We met when he came into the shop to ask permission to put up a poster for an event they are arranging in the city centre..."

"Yeah, and your dad gave me a hard time, he did," laughed Imran. "He wanted to be sure it wasn't something political, that we weren't holding any anti-war rallies or supporting terrorism..."

"We have to be careful, you know," explained his father, in a tone Faraz recognised as his 'sensible elder' voice. "Nowadays, you never know who is watching – and you young people have no sense. You end up causing trouble for all the Muslims in this country..." He carried on talking while Imran gave Faraz a knowing look as if to say 'These oldies, eh?'

Faraz smiled. This guy seemed all right. "What was the poster about then?"

"We have a Muslim arts organisation and we're putting together a programme for the youth, you know, keep them off the streets and all that..."

Faraz's eyes lit up and he was about to ask for more details when they heard the *imam* clearing his throat, the sound amplified by the mike at the front of the room.

Imran signalled that he would talk to him after the prayer and melted into the row behind.

"*Allahu akbar!*"

The *tarawih* prayers had begun.

Faraz tried hard to concentrate on the Arabic words that flowed from the *imam's* mouth. There was no denying that he was a skilful reciter: his melodies were beautiful, his tone pitch perfect. But Faraz wished, more than ever, that he could actually understand the words, that he could grasp their meaning. He knew that this was *Surah al-Baqarah*, the Verse of the Cow, because tonight was the first night of Ramadan, and the recitation always started from the beginning of the *Qur'an*. But beyond that, he was clueless, picking up only a few familiar words. What was the point of memorising the *Qur'an* at *madressah* if you couldn't even understand it at the end?

This is rubbish, he thought to himself. *If I come again, I am going to read the English translation first.*

After a while, he stopped straining to decipher the meaning and began to lose himself in the moment, in the movements of the prayer, in the emotion in the *imam's* voice as he spoke of Paradise and Hell-fire, of guidance and loss. Faraz found his spirits lift even as his feet grew sore from standing for so long. He was in the zone. He could have stayed there all night.

But, after about an hour, the *imam* led the last *tasleem*.

"*Asalaamu alaikum warahmatullah*," to the right shoulder. "*Asalaamu alaikum warahmatullah*," to the left shoulder. And it was over.

Tomorrow, they would all be fasting and the strong would come again tomorrow night and the next night and the next.

Faraz hoped to be one of them.

Tired but content, he waited with his father for the mosque to empty slightly before they too got up to leave. As he was putting on his shoes, Imran came up behind him.

"*Asalaamu alaikum*, bro," he said, his voice lower, calmer now than before the prayer. "We didn't get to finish our conversation. Here's a flyer, that's my mobile number, there. You can call me or visit our website if you want to know more about what we do. Take care, yeah?"

And he was gone.

Faraz felt the texture of the card, grainy beneath his fingers, and noticed the same 'Islamic urban' art theme to it. He made a mental note to check out the website as soon as he got home.

On the way home, father and son did not speak, each lost in his own thoughts. Faraz thought of Auntie Naj and the book she had given him. He felt sure that it was her advice and what he had read in the book that had enabled him to 'feel' that night's prayer, in a way he never had before.

★ ★ ★

Faraz and his father arrived home to find the house tidy and warm. Ammiji had gone to sleep but Farhana was upstairs in her room, still awake.

Faraz knocked on her door after saying goodnight to his dad. He found her lying in bed reading, her head propped up on one hand.

"Hey, sis," he said, pulling up a chair.

"Hey," she said, looking up at him briefly. "How was the prayer?"

"It was all right…" He knew then that she was still upset about not being able to go. "What did you and Ammiji get up to?"

Farhana raised her eyebrows at him.

"What do you *think*?" Her voice was harsh, bitter. "We tidied up after dinner, washed up and prepared the food to cook tomorrow, same as always!"

He didn't know what to say so he just looked at her, waiting to see if she would go on. And she did.

"It's just not fair, Faraz!" she cried, taking care not to speak loud enough for their dad to hear. "That's all I ever see women doing in our family during Ramzan: cooking and cleaning, cooking and cleaning! What's the point? I thought we were supposed to be in this together, that we were supposed to be worshipping too. But instead, we're busier than ever with the mundane stuff, the stupid details, the food, food, food!"

"OK, sis, easy, it's not that bad…you get reward for that too, remember?"

"Oh, Faraz!" she snapped impatiently,

"You don't understand, you'll never understand. You're a guy, you're free to go mosque, come back whatever time, read *Qur'an* all day if you want. Do you know that Ammiji has *never* been to pray *tarawih* in the mosque? Ever in her life?"

Faraz squirmed slightly. "Ammiji always says it's not really our culture; women just don't go mosque…"

"Well, bollocks to that!" Farhana's face was flushed and she threw her book down in frustration. "Ammiji may be happy to stay at home making *paneer* but I don't plan to waste this Ramzan cooking and cleaning – I want to make the most of every day, of every second…"

Faraz recognised that sentiment. He had felt the same way after reading the book that Auntie Najma had given him.

"And what's all that about women not going to the mosque? Auntie Naj goes all the time. The women during the Prophet's time used to go, so why shouldn't we?"

Faraz had never thought about it before. "Well, I guess that's just not part of Pakistani culture…"

"Yeah, and I thought it was Islam we followed!" Farhana tossed her hair defiantly. "Well, I'm just going to go with Auntie Najma – and I don't care what Ammiji or Dad say…"

"OK, sis, take it easy with the negativity, yeah? Tomorrow we'll be fasting – don't forget what that means. Is an argument about going mosque really worth it?"

He waited for her to answer.

Farhana's shoulders slumped.

"I guess not," she sighed at last. "It's just so frustrating, Faraz! Ammiji and I, it's like we speak a different language… like she doesn't understand anything that makes sense to me…"

"You have to remember that she didn't grow up here, sis, that's probably why. Pakistani culture is what she knows, what she understands. You know she adores you…"

"No, Faraz," Farhana interrupted. "She loves me, yes, but she adores *you*. You know you're her golden boy!"

"Look, all I know is there are some things you can tell your parents and some things you just can't. They've got their ideals, their expectations, and that's what they're interested in. They love us, of course, but that doesn't mean they are going to change for us. They know best. That's how it was for them and their parents and..."

"And miraculously things haven't changed, even though we were born and bred in the UK? Sounds crazy to me!"

"But we're living the craziness, sis, cos you know there is no other way."

Farhana thought about her split personality, her school persona and her character at home. Yup, she was living the craziness for sure.

Then she looked up at Faraz, a small smile on her face. "The prayer was good, wasn't it?"

He nodded, unable to suppress his grin.

"Yeah, I can tell. You seem different. Calmer, somehow. Like you've got it all figured out..."

"Well, I've figured out that I need to get to grips with the translation of the Arabic – and take a high energy snack before going: those *rakats* are tiring, man!"

They both laughed and the tension that had flooded the room only moments earlier dissipated.

Then Farhana yawned, her hand fluttering in front of her mouth. "It's late, Faraz. We'd better get some sleep."

"No doubt! It's only a few hours till *sehri* time. Good night, sis."

Farhana snuggled under her bedclothes and reached for the light switch.

"Goodnight, Faraz."

Click. Her light was out.

Faraz got up and made his way to the door. His sister's voice reached him through the dark.

"Faraz?"

"Yeah?"

"Thanks, yeah?"

"No problem, sis, no problem."

And he closed the door softly behind him.

Chapter 8

First fast

The clear skies did not last the night. By the time the twins' mum woke them up for *sehri*, they could hear the steady patter of rain outside.

Ammiji had been up for at least an hour before everyone else. Putting on her favourite grey jumper and fluffy slippers, she had turned on the heating, and set the table in preparation for that special first meal of the fasting day.

This had always been a labour of love for her, just as it had been for her own mother back home in Pakistan, who had always cooked for seven or more.

There were few things that she found as satisfying as watching her family eat good food she had prepared. For some reason, during Ramadan, this was even more important to her.

She decided to start things off properly, with *pakhoras*. They were Faraz's favourite and she only ever made them on special occasions. And then she began to prepare the fried eggs, baked beans, milky tea – Faraz and his father liked to eat well in the morning before fasting. Faraz in particular needed to keep his food intake up, especially if he was going to maintain his weight throughout Ramadan. He would have to have his regular protein shake before dawn too, just to top himself up.

Farhana, on the other hand, was more like her mother, and couldn't handle more than a bowl of cereal and juice, even before a day of fasting. She always said she couldn't eat so early in the morning.

Ammiji tiptoed up to her children's rooms, first Faraz's, then Farhana's, and shook them awake gently. They rose sleepily, arms stretching, hands fluttering to suppress yawns. She was overtaken by a wave of emotion.

"Come on, *beta*," she whispered to each of them in turn. "It's time to eat."

At first, the family ate together in silence, still heavy with sleep cut too short and stomachs that were not used to food so early in the morning. But, in that silence, and the silence of the street outside, there was camaraderie, a secret knowledge that other families like theirs were also awake, eating, gaining strength for the day of fasting that lay ahead.

But gradually, the sleepiness wore off and excitement bubbled up. At one point, Farhana almost giggled, she was so excited. And she laughed out loud when she saw Faraz preparing one of his protein shakes. Her brother's transformation from a skinny young boy to a muscle-bound lad never ceased to amaze or amuse her. It was as if she turned around one day and there they were: a young woman and a young man.

But he still had the same eyes, so soft and full of feeling and a smile that could reduce you to tears. Although she knew that Faraz sometimes resented his pretty-boy features, she hoped he would never lose the tenderness in those beautiful green eyes or the brightness of his smile.

My little brother, she smiled to herself. And she giggled again as he grimaced at the pink sludge he was now draining from a tall glass. The price to be paid, eh?

All too soon, the *azan* clock rang, reminding them that the time for *Fajr*, the morning prayer, had begun. No more eating now, until sunset. They all uttered a blessing – *'Alhamdulillah'* – and went to get ready to pray, some to the bathroom upstairs, others to the downstairs toilet.

Farhana looked at her face in the hallway mirror, framed by the scarf she always used when she prayed at home. She smiled. She didn't look that bad.

They prayed together in the front room, on mats that Ammiji had stretched out over the worn carpet. This was a rare treat, the family all praying together. They listened attentively as Dad recited from the shorter, more familiar verses at the end of the *Qur'an* and realised, to their surprise, that the last time they had heard him recite had been a year ago, last Ramadan.

Why do we have to wait until Ramzan to pray together? thought Faraz as his forehead touched the floor.

Just two *rakats* and the morning prayer was over. The family sat quietly, mouthing their *dhikr*, counting remembrance on their fingers: *subhanAllah, alhamdulillah, Allahu akbar.*

Farhana looked at her watch. It was still only 5:30am. Time for a few more hours of sleep before school. Except that she didn't feel like sleeping. She looked over at Faraz. He looked just as wide-awake as she did.

But Ammiji was already pulling up the mats, taking off the garment she always wore for *namaz*. Dad was on his way out of the living room.

"You going back to bed, Dad?" Farhana asked.

"Yes, *beta*, we've got a busy day at the shop today. You two should get some rest too or you'll be tired at school."

"I feel fine, Dad," said Faraz. "What about you, Ammiji?"

"I'm going to tidy up now, Faraz, the dishes don't wash themselves, you know?"

Farhana jumped up. "No, Ammiji, you go to sleep. I'll wash up. I don't feel tired anyway."

Her mother looked at her, surprised. "Are you sure, Farhana? You don't have to, you know…"

"It's OK, you go get some rest, go on."

They could soon hear their parents making their way up the stairs.

Faraz looked at his sister, impressed. "Not bad, sis!" he said. "Scoring points in the first hour of the fast, eh?"

Farhana looked at him and smiled wryly. "Don't worry, I won't be alone: get in that kitchen!"

Faraz tried to protest but Farhana bullied him all the way into the kitchen.

"Right, you clear up, I'll wash the dishes."

"Oh, all right then." Faraz was sheepish as he set about the unfamiliar task of stacking the plates and gathering up the cups.

Farhana put on a tape of *Qur'anic* recitation then filled the sink with hot water and was soon elbow-deep in bubbles and *sehri* dishes.

Faraz looked over at her. "It suits you, y'know," he murmured.

Farhana turned to him, puzzled, wondering what he was talking about. Then she touched her hand to her head and realised that she had not taken off her scarf. She bit her lip.

"D'you really think so?"

"Yeah, I do... I always have. I think girls look much better with *hijab*, to be honest."

"That's not really the point though, is

it?" Farhana replied crossly. Then her frown disappeared. "I'm thinking of wearing it full-time, y'know…"

"Yeah, sis, go for it… keep those guys in line, I say!"

"OK," said Farhana, rolling her eyes, "let's get one thing straight. If I was to wear *hijab*, it wouldn't be for any guy. I think that is so lame; it doesn't even make a difference these days anyway. Guys still hit on you and stuff…"

"That's true…" murmured Faraz, thinking of how he felt about Shazia, in spite of her scarf.

"Anyway," continued his sister, "the *hijab*, *if* I decide to wear it, will be *my* decision, and mine alone – and I don't really care what anyone else thinks of it!"

"I don't think Ammiji will like it…" Faraz frowned. Although Ammiji always wore a long shawl, a *dupatta*, draped across her shoulders or perched on top of her head when attending religious gatherings, they both knew that she considered the headscarf and other Islamic clothing unnecessary and alien to the Islam she grew up with.

Farhana sighed. "I know, Faraz, I know. She's told me so often enough. But this is something

I w███████g for me, between me and Allah.
I wo██████at she would understand that..."

"*Insha-Allah*," replied Faraz, still doubtful.

They both fell silent. When Faraz had finished wiping the table down, he got his copy of the *Qur'an* in English and began to read the meaning of *Surat-ul-Baqarah*, the Verse of the Cow. Farhana joined him as soon as she was finished and, being the faster reader, waited patiently for him to finish reading the page before turning it over.

On the other side of the kitchen curtains, the sky began to brighten slowly. Daylight found brother and sister sitting at the kitchen table, reading, their heads almost touching, a translation of the *Qur'an* lying between them.

★ ★ ★

Somehow, both Faraz and Farhana made it through that first day. Having had little sleep and with bellies that began to rumble and throats that began to ache as the day wore on, they managed to fast for the whole day.

At Farhana's school, Shazia and many of the other girls were fasting too, so the experience was communal. At lunchtime, ████████ the classroom that the school had assig████ █ayers for the Muslim students and prayed th██ together, united by the unexpected bond of hunger and sacrifice.

But in spite of the hunger, the mood was buoyant, and the girls laughed and chatted, talking about what they would eat for *iftar*, for *sehri* the next day, their plans for Eid. Farhana told Shazia about Faraz's protein shake, at which Shazia laughed out loud.

"He's changed so much, he has!" Shazia still remembered him, her best mate's twin brother, all scrawny and timid, unable to say two words without stammering.

He wasn't like that any more.

Farhana and Shazia had been best friends since nursery school. They lived in the same neighbourhood; their parents attended the same mosque and were good friends. Shazia's dad, the local *imam*, was highly respected in the neighbourhood and his family was considered a 'good family'. Farhana's parents were proud to count them as their friends.

"You know what, Shaz?" Farhana said softly

during a lull in the conversation. "I don't know what it is, but I feel different this Ramzan. Like I'm on the edge of something major, something life-changing... I haven't felt like that before, not about Ramzan."

"Well, you know what it's like - we've been fasting since primary school, haven't we? It's just a part of life now."

"But that's just what I mean, Shazia, it doesn't feel like other years. I've been talking a lot to my auntie you see..."

"You mean the one who used to live in London? The one who covers up and everything?"

"Yeah, that's right, my Auntie Naj. She's given me a lot to think about, y' see."

"Yeah? Like what?"

"Well, I've been praying all my five prayers for a little while now as you know, trying to learn a bit more. And, of course, I'm going to try and fast properly, not that rubbish we did last year..."

Shazia giggled guiltily, remembering their secret trips to the fish 'n' chips shop during school break time, hiding in the alley so that the Muslim guys from the curry shop across the road wouldn't see them and tell her dad.

Farhana took a deep breath and continued. "And another thing: I'm thinking of wearing the *hijab*. Just trying it, you know, for Ramzan. I reckon I might as well give it a go."

Shazia stared at her friend, a look of horror on her face.

"What are you going to do a thing like that for?" she gasped.

"Shazia!"

"I'm serious! Just how do you think Miss Farhana Ahmed, the queen of the Bollywood Massive, head of Class H and and all-round hottie is going to wear the scarf? Do you have any idea what it will mean for your social life? What the other girls will say? What *Robina* will say?"

"Yeah, I have thought about all that, you know!"

"I don't think you have, love! Do you really think that you can commit to something as major as that? And what about Malik? What will he think?"

Farhana's face darkened. "Don't talk about him – there's nothing there. I can't make my life decisions based on what *he* thinks."

"So he never did call and apologise then," Shazia murmured.

Farhana shook her head and bit her lip, tears stinging her eyes. Malik's betrayal still hurt, a full three months later.

"Well, I'm just thinking about it. I haven't decided yet. And how can *you* go on like that? You wear scarf, don't you?"

"Yeah, but only because Dad makes me!" Shazia retorted. "It's just that all the women in my family cover – we're the *imam's* family, after all! Personally, I don't really think I need to. It's not like I'm a great looker or anything. Anyway, I don't have time for boys and all that stuff."

Farhana shook her head. "There you go, talking that rubbish again. I just wish you would look in the mirror and see what everybody else sees!"

"What, a fat Paki with four eyes?" Shazia snorted.

"No, you daft thing! A bright, intelligent, beautiful, voluptuous, curvaceous, bootilicious…"

"Oh, cut it out, will yer!" Shazia slapped Farhana with her school bag. "Hey, there goes the bell - we'd better leg it!"

The two girls grabbed their bags and hurried towards the East Block, where one of Farhana's favourite classes, English Literature, was about to start.

* * *

Faraz's experience was slightly different. Unlike his sister, he had never been surrounded by a group of mates, all into what he was into, all interested in what he had to say.

He went to the Muslim prayer room at lunch time though, to pray and to see who else was fasting. There were quite a few boys there, ones he had seen at the mosque the night before. Again, they nodded their greetings and uttered brief 'salaams' before performing their prayers. Most of the boys left straight afterwards. Some stayed briefly to read from mini *Qur'ans*. These were the religious boys – the outcasts.

After a little while, however, Faraz found himself all alone in the makeshift prayer room. He was happy to be there, out of trouble, but he was bored. He fished around in his school bag and his fingers felt a scratchy piece of card. He pulled it out. It was that brother Imran's business card. He glanced up at the wall clock. If he hurried, and if the computer room wasn't too busy, he might be able to check out the website before the next bell went.

He grabbed his bag and bolted out of the door.

The computer room was pretty full but, to his relief, he saw a single empty workstation and hurried towards it. Once he had logged on to the Internet, he quickly typed in the web address on the card.

The site took a while to load. But gradually the screen began to fill with images, 'urban Islamic' images, just like Imran's t-shirt. Faraz could feel himself growing more and more excited as he saw the artwork slideshow. Graffiti using Arabic letters loomed large on various city walls, huge canvases of geometric designs in bright, eclectic colours, galleries showcasing different artists' work, and the t-shirts and hoodies emblazoned with similar themes.

He read the blurb: an urban Islamic arts movement, dedicated to excellence and innovation in art and a commitment to community.

Sounds amazing, thought Faraz. *Absolutely amazing.*

There was one artist in particular whose work kept drawing his eye. He saw a partial photo: an Asian guy, big, beard, but dressed just like a street thug, with a spray can in his hand, standing in front of a huge mural on a Birmingham city wall: 'salaam' it read.

This guy had done murals all over the world, been on the BBC, exhibited in Dubai. Faraz felt a stab of envy.

I wonder what his family think of him doing a crazy job like that?

His dad had often said that he hoped that Faraz would take over the newsagent's and, certainly, it was what the rest of the family expected, especially since he wouldn't be going to university. 'No, Faraz is not the university type,' he had heard his mum say more than once.

But seeing this Muslim graffiti artist, *desi* like him, getting on with it, staying true to his identity while living life as an artist, gave him a surge of hope.

Maybe there was a way he could still please everybody… just maybe….

Chapter 9

Breaking the fast

That night, they all went to Naneeji's for *iftar*.

Ammiji, Farhana and Faraz had already broken their fast with dates at home while they waited for Dad to get back from the mosque after sunset prayers. He had closed the shop early in honour of the first day of Ramadan and, soon enough, they heard his car creak to a stop outside.

After swallowing down another protein shake, Faraz helped his mum and Farhana carry the hot containers of *pakhoras*, *biryani* and lamb curry, his mum's speciality, to the car. She had been busy all afternoon, as had her sisters and sisters-in-law and, when they got to Naneeji's house, it was clear that there was enough food to feed a small army.

The little terraced house where Naneeji had lived for the past fifteen years since her husband had passed away was full to bursting with three generations. Naneeji's sister Razia was there with her son and daughter, their children, as well as her own children and grandchildren, sons-in-law and daughters-in-law.

After greeting everyone, Farhana took off her coat and joined her aunties in the kitchen, preparing the dishes to be served to the men who were waiting in the front room.

Her younger cousins flitted in and out of the lounge and the kitchen, snatching bites of *samosas* and onion bhaji, high on the adrenaline they could feel from the adults.

The women worked quickly – the men were clearly hungry because their voices couldn't be heard above the racket that the children were making.

As soon as the men had been served, Farhana's mum and aunts began to dish up for themselves and the children.

It was Auntie Najma and Farhana's job to take all the little ones to the bathroom to wash their hands and, by the time they got back to the living room, the floor mat was down and the trays of food were being brought through. Auntie Najma slipped quietly back to the kitchen.

Almost faint with hunger, Farhana sat down at last and took her first mouthful of proper food since the night before.

Bismillah...

Silence descended on the house as everyone ate from communal trays on the floor, right hands picking up curry and masala with *roti*, dipping in *raita*, collecting every rice grain.

Food never tastes as good as after a day of fasting, thought Farhana. She saw the same sentiment echoed on the faces of all around her.

She looked with admiration at Naneeji and her sister-in-law, who was also her cousin, their chiffon *dupattas* covering grey and hennaed hair, both of them approaching their seventies, still fasting Ramadan, still cooking for their ever-growing families.

Farhana felt her heart swell with joy and satisfaction. She had done it! She had fasted the whole day! And she felt sure that she had kept her promises to herself about staying on the right track.

Malik hadn't called or texted today – he was probably fasting too and felt too guilty to call her up. It was probably just as well –

less temptation that way.

Soon enough, the men were talking about needing more food. Auntie Sajda and Ammiji got up and went to the kitchen to empty the containers, sending through more food. They would all be in a hurry now, to catch the night prayers at the mosque, then *tarawih*.

Uncle Munir's wife, Asma, put on a pan of milk to make sweet cardamom tea.

"Where is Najma?" asked Auntie Anisa's husband, Uncle Ali.

Auntie Anisa rolled her eyes. "Oh, *she* won't eat with us! Not with you and Abid here – says you are not related to her, that it is not allowed."

Uncle Ali laughed, his big belly quivering slightly. "Tell her we won't bite!" Then he shouted through the open door: "Najma-ji, it's OK, we won't bite!"

"I know, Ali-bhai, I know!" came the voice from the kitchen. But Auntie Najma didn't enter the room until all the men had gone. Only then did she hang up her *abayah* and scarf.

"*Asalaamu alaikum*, honey," said Auntie Najma, leaning over to fold up the floor mat. "How was your first day?"

Farhana sat back on her heels and smiled broadly.

"It was fine, *masha Allah*! Much easier than I expected it to be..."

"That's great! And how is Faraz doing?"

"He seems good, too," replied Farhana. "We stayed up after *Fajr* actually, read some *Qur'an* together... it was nice..."

"Ahh, that sounds lovely, *masha Allah*!" Auntie Najma's face glowed with pleasure. "So glad to see the two of you getting into it. Did you pray *tarawih* last night?"

Farhana's face darkened momentarily. "No," she frowned. "Dad and Faraz went but Ammiji said I had to stay home and help her in the house."

Auntie Najma lifted an eyebrow. "Ah, yes, of course... that mosque is mainly for men, isn't it?" There was more than a touch of irony in her voice. "But you could still have prayed at home, you know..."

"I guess so, I suppose I was just too upset about not being able to go – I will try to remember that next time though."

"You should come with me next time I go,"

said Auntie Najma, getting up to put the mats away. "I go to a mosque about 25 minutes from here – they have loads of space for women and the recitation is beautiful."

"Oh, could I, Auntie?" Farhana's face lit up.

"In fact, why don't you come to *iftar* with me this weekend? One of my friends invited me – I met her at uni – I think you would like her... you haven't really met my friends, have you?"

"No," replied Farhana, "but Ammiji is convinced that they are a bad influence – I mean, look at what happened to you!"

They both laughed good-naturedly.

"So, will you come?"

"I'm not sure, Auntie. I think I would feel funny meeting your friends. They're all *niqabis* and *hijabis*, aren't they?"

"So?" said Auntie Najma, indignantly. "What's that got to do with anything?"

"Well, I don't want them to judge me, you know, cos I don't wear *hijab*..."

"That is a load of rubbish! Anyone who judges you without getting to know you isn't worth knowing in the first place. Besides, my friends are cool, they aren't like that."

"You'd have to ask Ammiji for me. She'll never let me go otherwise."

"Don't you worry, I'll speak to her. So, it's a date, is it?"

Farhana smiled. "I guess so…"

Auntie Najma winked at her and got up to assess the damage in the front room, where the children were watching TV.

Farhana smiled to herself, then got up to go to the kitchen.

As she reached the kitchen doorway, she heard a low but tense-sounding conversation taking place and then her mum's voice rose above all the others. "Najma has always been selfish, everyone knows that!"

This was greeted by a chorus of fierce whispers which came to an abrupt halt when she stepped into the kitchen. Farhana's mum breathed in sharply and quickly turned away to sweep the leftovers into the bin. Auntie Sajda sighed and ran a cloth over the counter in front of her, a frown etched between her eyebrows. Naneeji turned and managed a watery smile in Farhana's direction while her great aunt Razia glared at no one in particular.

It was clear that she had interrupted something and, by the sounds of it, it was something serious to do with Auntie Najma.

What could she have done now?

★ ★ ★

That night, both Faraz and Farhana prayed *tarawih*.

Faraz stood in the first row behind the *imam*, next to his dad, his body bowing and prostrating with a sea of others. This time, he was more aware of the meanings behind the beautiful words that flowed from the *imam's* mouth. He had read the English translation that morning and appreciated the meanings of each verse of the *Qur'an*. They spoke to him and he responded to the words as never before.

He mentally swept away thoughts of school, of home, of every detail that could distract him from his prayer.

And when he knelt with his face to the green carpet of the mosque, he prayed his own private prayers, fervently, passionately, asking for forgiveness, asking for everything his heart desired, asking for strength and guidance.

When he and Dad came back to Naneeji's house to pick up Ammiji and Farhana, he felt he had been washed clean, fresh and sparkling.

So this is what gives those mosque boys that glow, he thought to himself with a smile.

It felt good.

★ ★ ★

Farhana also prayed *tarawih,* with Auntie Najma, by lamplight in her aunt's room. The room smelt of perfume and books and the streets outside were still.

Auntie Najma's gravelly voice lost its edge when she recited *Qur'an.* Her recitation was slow and deliberate, powerful and moving, coaxing tears from Farhana's eyes. She and her aunt raised their hands, their feet and shoulders pressed together. They were so close, Farhana could feel her aunt's body shudder when she recited certain verses, verses that brought her to tears and interrupted her recitation.

Farhana shut out the world and lost herself in the prayer. She wanted to pray as if she was standing before Allah, as if she could see Him, knowing that He could see her.

In that prayer, she asked for forgiveness for all past wrongs, for every slip-up, for every oversight, every sin. She poured her heart out and let repentance in. And she emerged from the *salah* cleansed, ready to move forward.

When they sat next to each other on the way home in the car, the twins did not need words. They both knew, almost instinctively, that that night was a turning point.

Chapter 10

Hijab

The first thing Farhana noticed when she stepped out of the house on the way to school the next morning was how warm her ears felt. She had left Faraz behind as he was running late. She wanted to get to school early this morning.

The white cotton was snug, not too tight, but close enough to frame her face and keep her hair from escaping.

She had tried many different styles and had settled on wearing the scarf low over her brow, rather than high up near her hairline as other girls did. It suited the shape of her face more and, strangely enough, emphasised her high cheekbones and the slight dimple in her chin.

You are so vain, Farhana, she told herself, and felt a stab of guilt. This was not a beauty accessory, like one of her many different hats or her fuchsia pashmina. This was worship. And that was just what she had tried to tell Ammiji when she had come down to breakfast in her scarf. Dad and Faraz were still upstairs getting dressed.

As soon as Ammiji had caught sight of her, she had taken a deep breath. "Farhana," she had said, "why are you dressed like that?"

Farhana was so taken aback by the irony of her mother's question that she almost laughed.

"Like what, Ammiji?" she had asked, trying to sound normal, but hating the look of fear and incomprehension in her mother's eyes.

"Like *that*!" Ammiji had raised her voice. "That is not part of your school uniform, is it? What are you trying to do? Cause a problem for your father and me with the school? Show everyone how religious you are?"

★ ★ ★

Shazia screamed when she recognised Farhana coming to meet her at the bus stop. "Oh my God!" she shrieked. "I can't believe you really did it! How do you feel?"

Farhana giggled. "Warm!"

They both started laughing.

"Has your mum seen you?"

Farhana nodded and bit her lip.

"What did she say?"

"She wasn't pleased, let me put it that way..."

That was an understatement.

"No, seriously, I feel good. I feel like it's the right thing to do and that now is the right time... does it make me look weird, though?"

"Well," said Shazia, putting her head to one side and eyeing her friend critically. "I must admit, it does suit you. It can really drain some girls but you, you're still stunning but in a really innocent way – makes your eyes look massive!"

"Well, I did tell Faraz that I wouldn't be doing it to look good – it has to be from the heart or it isn't worth it, is it?"

"Depends on whether you have a choice or not, I guess," murmured Shazia ruefully.

"What do you mean, Shaz?"

"Look, Farhana, I've told you before, the only reason I wear scarf is that my dad would go ballistic if I ever tried to leave the house without it. As far as he's concerned, Muslim girls must wear scarf, end of story, case closed. And I know that he's right, but he never appreciates how I feel about it..."

"But you're just doing what I should have been doing all along..."

"Yeah, but it's different, see? You know what it's like to have guys tell you you're pretty, to fancy you. I may never have that..."

Farhana looked down, thinking of the many tears she had shed over Malik. "Believe me, Shaz, it's not all that great. It really isn't. Sometimes I envy you because you've been protected from so much rubbish, stuff that we did that we knew we shouldn't really be doing. And I see that now. I think you should rethink your reasons for wearing *hijab* – it's your life, remember? You only get one chance..."

"Yeah, I guess so... still, would be nice to know that there is someone out there who could see something in me. But I guess that's life, isn't it? Come on, here's the bus."

As the two girls boarded their bus, they didn't notice Faraz coming up the path. Next to a tree, he stopped, just hidden from view, and watched them as they disappeared up the stairs.

★ ★ ★

That first day in *hijab* was strange for Farhana.

On the one hand, she felt really pleased that she had had the guts to actually put it on and come to school. Some of the other Muslim girls congratulated her, asking her how she learnt to tie it like that, when she started, how she felt. These were the religious girls, the quiet ones, the ones who weren't allowed to attend most school functions, the ones everyone ignored. She didn't want to become like them but she admired their quiet faith and their gentle manners. She would do well to spend a bit more time with them.

On the other hand, she had to deal with the incredulous looks and comments from some of the other girls.

Robina was fulsome in her disdain. When she saw Farhana in the first lesson, she rolled her eyes dramatically.

"Oh, not you too, Farhana, honestly! I know you've been hanging with that auntie of yours but there's no need to go all extreme!" That got a laugh out of some of the other girls, Robina's party people. "And just because Malik dumped you doesn't mean you need to go all Islamic on us…"

Her corner of the room erupted. "Oooohhh, you didn't go *there*, Robina?"

Farhana looked at Robina then - a long, searching look. *Remind me why we are friends*, she thought to herself.

"For your information," she said at last, taking her seat, "this was my decision. It doesn't have anything to do with anyone else, OK?"

One of the white girls, Clara, piped up: "I think it looks really great on you, Farhana. I bet it was a tough decision to make..."

Farhana smiled at her gratefully.

"But why, Farhana?" one of the other non-Muslim girls asked. "Is it cos it's the month of Ramadan?"

"To be honest, I've been thinking about it for a while now – and I feel ready..."

"Ready to become a social outcast, you mean," snorted Robina. "Honestly, Farhana, you have everything going for you! Why throw it all away just so that people think you're a bit religious? My sister reckons most girls who wear scarf are hypocrites anyway. They want everyone to think that they're all Islamic but they're up to all sorts. I mean, it's fine if you want to play that 'good religious girl' game but it takes more guts to just do what you like anyway, regardless of what people think of you."

"Is that what your sister says?" asked Farhana.

"Yeah it is, and she should know. She does whatever the hell she likes and she doesn't give a damn about what 'the community' thinks. I ain't never gonna live my life according to what people think I should and shouldn't do – life's too short for that, eh, girls?"

"Innit, tho!" There was loud agreement from Robina's friends, but thoughtful silence from the rest of the girls.

Farhana burned with frustration. She wanted to grab Robina by her arms and shake her, make her see sense. She was a Muslim, wasn't she? How come that didn't count for anything? But how could she turn around and start preaching now? It would sound too ridiculous coming from her so, for the first time in a long while, she backed down from a debate.

"Well, if it makes you feel any better, this isn't about what people will think of me. It's about my own journey, my faith. And especially in this month, in Ramzan, that is something we should all be thinking about…"

The other girls fell silent then, and as their English teacher, Ms Robinson, walked into the room, they returned to their seats and straightened their tables.

Ms Robinson greeted the girls, then proceeded to hand out the essays she had been marking over the weekend.

"Farhana Ahmed?" She glanced up, expecting to see the green eyes and glossy black hair that she had grown accustomed to over the year. It took her a moment to register that the girl in the white scarf was Farhana. She raised an eyebrow.

"Yes, Miss?" came the reply.

"Farhana? You look... different..."

"She's on her way to a *burqa*, Miss!" cried out one of the girls, and Robina's crew cracked up.

Ms Robinson smiled indulgently. "I'm sure Farhana is much too smart to end up in a *burqa*, aren't you, Farhana?"

Farhana was taken aback. A quizzical expression crossed her face. *What was that all about?*

"Sorry, Miss?"

"Oh, nothing, Farhana, nothing at all..."

Something inside Farhana's head shifted into gear. She recognised it from her many hours spent on the debate team. She wasn't going down without a fight. This English class had been a battleground many times. Ms Robinson encouraged the girls to express themselves freely and openly challenged them to defend their arguments and ideas.

"Miss," she began coolly, "do you think that the way a woman dresses makes her more or less intelligent?"

"No, of course not," was her teacher's response. "Every woman has the right to dress the way she wants."

"And do you see nuns as oppressed?"

"No, of course not, that's their choice…"

"So is choice the issue then? What if a woman chooses to wear a scarf? Or a *burqa*, for that matter? Does that make *her* oppressed?"

"Well, the crucial issue here is choice and the fact is that many Muslim women don't have a ch…"

"Is that an assumption, Miss? Or a fact?"

Pause. Several girls shifted in their seats, waiting to see where this discussion was going.

"An assumption, I suppose…"

"Exactly! So what if an intelligent, educated, ambitious woman decides, of her own volition, to wear a scarf, is she any less intelligent than a woman who doesn't wear one?"

"Well, Farhana, it was merely a passing comment…"

"Well, Miss, I take issue with the fact that you or anyone else is prepared to judge the level of my intelligence by what I choose to wear on my head. I think it's wrong, just as I think it's wrong to judge you or any other woman by the length of your skirt. Wouldn't you agree?"

Several girls broke out into cheers as Ms Robinson smiled and nodded her head, prepared to concede the point.

"Fair enough, Farhana, you've made your point. Now, can I get on with handing out these essays?"

"See that, Miss," called Clara, "she's still cheeky, scarf or no scarf!"

Farhana grinned, her cheeks burning. That was more like it. One thing was for sure: the scarf wasn't going to stand in the way of her being herself at school. She was still Farhana Ahmed, after all.

And don't you forget it, she thought, smiling at the A grade on her latest essay.

Chapter 11

A way forward

Faraz could hardly concentrate in class that morning and, the first free moment he had, he rang the number on Imran's card.

The phone rang about six times before anyone picked up.

"Hello… *asalaamu alaikum*," began Faraz, rather hesitantly. He was not used to calling up virtual strangers and he felt the sweat break out beneath his collar.

"*Wa alaikum salaam*," replied the voice on the other end.

"Imran?" Faraz was fairly sure it was him but didn't want to make a fool of himself.

"Yes, this is Imran," came the response. "Who's this?"

"Err, it's Faraz… we met at the mosque the

other night... me dad owns the newsagent's in Harcourt Street?"

"Ah, yes, of course!" The recognition in his voice was unmistakable. Faraz breathed a sigh of relief and wiped the sweat from the back of his neck.

"How're you doing, bro?" Imran asked.

"Yeah, I'm fine... listen, I had a look at your website at school yesterday." Faraz had never been one for small talk.

"Uh huh?"

"And I thought it looked brilliant... just brilliant."

"Ah, great, glad you liked it... are you interested in anything in particular?"

"Well, I love art, y'see, all kinds. And I really liked the Arabic graffiti guy – what's his name again?"

"Oh, you mean Ahmed Ali? Yeah, he is very talented, *masha Allah*...You into graffiti?"

"Well, I've done some pieces at school, nothing serious, nothing on any walls or anything..."

"Would you like to see Ahmed Ali at work?"

Faraz's eyes widened. He could hardly believe his ears. "Of course! I mean, yes, yes, I would!"

"Well, it just so happens that he will be spraying a mural in the town centre day after tomorrow. It's part of our Ramadan Awareness programme. Why don't you come along? I could introduce you to him."

Faraz fumbled for a pen and wrote down the name of the building and what time Ahmed Ali would be there. His heart pounded in his chest and he could hardly contain his excitement. He would definitely be there the day after tomorrow, *insha Allah*.

"OK, bro, I have to go. Will you be at *tarawih* prayers tonight?" asked Imran.

"Yes, *insha Allah*, I hope so... see you later then, maybe?"

"Yeah, *insha Allah*, see you later. And if not, then tomorrow, OK?"

"OK!"

Imran rang off.

Faraz could hardly wait for the day to end. It was only the thought of Mr McCarthy's lesson at the end of the day that kept him going.

Just before going back to class, he sent his sister a text message: *Salam. Meet me aftr skool. Fraz.*

★ ★ ★

Faraz was bursting with anticipation as he waited for Farhana at the bus stop. When at last she arrived, he did a double take. He hadn't seen her in her *hijab* in the morning.

"Hey, sis," he smiled, "looking good! How did the girls at school take your new look?"

"Hmm, so-so," replied Farhana, adjusting her scarf. "Nothing Miss Farhana Ahmed can't handle."

Faraz chuckled. "That's my girl!"

"What's up anyway, Faraz, where are we going?"

"I've just got to show you this Muslim artist's work, man! It will blow your mind!"

"We're going to an art gallery?"

"Nah, this guy uses the street as his gallery. Come on, this bus will take us there. I'll fill you in on the way…"

Pleased to see her brother so animated, Farhana followed him into the bus.

By the time they got down to the building whose name Faraz had scribbled down, there was a small crowd gathering. They began to ease their way to the front.

In front of them loomed a large wall at the end of a row of shops. The wall and its surroundings had seen better days, that was for sure. Faraz scanned the figures in front of the wall and immediately spotted Ahmed Ali. He was as big and burly as he was in his pictures and he wore dark glasses. Several spray cans poked out of his army jacket pockets.

At that moment, he was standing back from the wall, his head on one side, looking at the rough silhouette he had already sprayed on to the ageing bricks, obviously trying to decide something.

"That's him over there," Faraz whispered to his sister, pointing him out.

Then, all of a sudden, Ahmed Ali sprang into action. Like a giant bumblebee, he began to flit and hover across the wall, leaving great swathes of colour in his wake. First the brighter colours, then the shades, then the dramatic black outlines that brought his Arabic letters and graffiti renditions to life. Then the finishing touches: the gloss on the lettering, the twinkles on the dark background, the glow on the motifs. The wall was transformed: it seemed to move and pulse with life, the smell of spray paints thick in the air.

The crowd gasped in appreciation of the image and the message: *shukr*, gratitude. Some of them applauded. The television cameras were there to capture the finished product and Ahmed Ali made a short speech, thanking the town for welcoming him and being such a great audience. Then Imran stepped up and said a few words, thanking the city council for granting permission to stage the event, telling the crowd about the Islamic urban art project.

Faraz thought he would burst with pride. *Brilliant*, he thought to himself again. He grinned over at his sister and saw that she was smiling too, her eyes alight. She reached for his hand and squeezed it.

She sees what I see, thought Faraz. *A future for me, doing what I love.*

"You go up there and you show him your stuff," she said, pushing him forward.

Faraz hesitated, but only for a moment. As the event came to a close and the crowd began to surge forward towards Ahmed Ali, he clutched his portfolio to his chest and made a beeline for Imran.

Imran saw him coming and a smile lit up his face.

"*Asalaamu alaikum*, bro, you made it!" They shook hands and embraced. "Is that your work in there?" he asked. Faraz nodded. Imran leaned over to Ahmed Ali and whispered in his ear. Ahmed looked across at Faraz and smiled at him.

"*Asalaamu alaikum*, bruv, be with you in a minute, yeah?" He was still busy signing autographs, responding to people's questions, making way for people to take photos of his latest mural.

"D'you mind if I have a look?" asked Imran, when it became clear that they would be waiting for a while.

Faraz jumped slightly, then nodded and haltingly handed his portfolio over to Imran. He turned away and busied himself with studying the freshly painted mural. He didn't want to see Imran's face as he looked through his work.

He heard the swish of the thick pages as Imran looked through his drawings, sketches, paintings and collages.

"*Masha Allah*, bro… wow…" There was no mistaking the admiration in his voice. Faraz turned to him finally, his face burning, and saw the look on Imran's face. He was clearly impressed.

"Ahmed's got to see this!" he cried and immediately walked over to Ahmed Ali who was saying goodbye to a reporter from the local paper.

"Bro, you have to see this young brother's work – it'll blow you away, *masha Allah*!"

Faraz watched Ahmed's face intently as he too leafed through the portfolio. He lingered on some pages longer than others, a smile touching his lips. Then he looked up at Faraz and grinned, his teeth bright against the dark hair of his bushy beard.

"You've got some real talent here, bruv, *masha Allah*! This stuff is really amazing... how old did you say you were?"

"Sixteen..." was Faraz's reply.

Ahmed turned to Imran. "You better sign this boy up quick, Imran. This is just the kind of young talent we need in the organisation, man." Then he turned back to Faraz. "I'm going down south next week but I'll be back in town in the last week of Ramadan to paint another mural – you handy with a spray can?"

Faraz nodded.

"Well, how would you like to come and paint the mural with me? It's on the wall of a school –

I can't remember the name now – but we're doing it with some lads from the area, y'know. Bridge-building and all that... what do you say?"

Faraz nodded. "Yeah, yeah, of course. That sounds brilliant..."

"Here's my card – that's my email address. You let me know for sure before the event, yeah? I can only have a limited number of lads on the wall with me at one time..."

Imran interrupted. "Don't worry, Ahmed, Faraz will be there. There's so much work to be done in the city, so much work with the youth. You see them out there, getting worse every day. It's like the streets are claiming them one by one..."

"I know, man, I used to be in that life, y'know... it's hard to resist, especially when you don't have anything to replace it."

"Well, hopefully, this is what we can do with the urban arts project: give them something to replace it..."

Faraz listened absently to their conversation. He saw himself in front of a wall, spray can in hand, bringing the bricks to life with colour. He grinned to himself. He could hardly wait!

"Listen, it'll be time to break fast soon – you coming to mine, Ahmed?"

"Nah, I promised the missus I would take her out to eat – she hasn't really seen much of this place."

"OK, then, we'd better get moving… Faraz?"

"Yeah, I'd better get home too, my sister's over there and our mum is expecting us."

The two men looked over briefly and lifted their hands in a semi-wave, a sort of long-distance 'salaam'.

Faraz started zipping up his portfolio. "I'll see you guys around, yeah? At the mosque, Imran?"

"*Insha Allah*," Imran answered as he shook Faraz's hand and embraced him again. "And keep up the good work, OK? I'll email you with the details of the next youth meeting…"

Faraz practically ran up to Farhana.

"So?" she asked, eagerly, "what did he say? What did he think?"

Faraz ducked his head shyly. "He reckons I've got talent, y'know? Wants me to work with them on their arts project, maybe even paint a wall with Ahmed Ali…"

"That is *brilliant*, Faraz!" Farhana was ecstatic.

"I'm so happy for you!" And she gave his arm a big squeeze.

"You're all right, you know that, sis? My best cheerleader…"

"Hey, that's what sisters are for!"

They both laughed as they saw their bus approach the bus stop and the sun start to sink behind the apartment buildings.

This was definitely shaping up to be the best Ramadan ever.

★ ★ ★

The twins woke before dawn and ate *sehri* with their mum and dad, the food delicious and filling, as usual.

Faraz was pleased that he had been able to maintain his weight in spite of the day's fasting and Farhana was happy with her weigh too, albeit for different reasons.

They prayed each morning as a family in their living room. Brother and sister now had an established ritual. When their parents went back to bed, they stayed up to read *Qur'an*, Faraz reading the verses that would be recited that evening at the mosque, Farhana reciting the Arabic alongside. She was determined to finish reading it during Ramadan this year. This and the shared breaking of the fast at sunset, the talks they would have every night, the emails their aunt sent them, brought them closer than they had been in a long time.

Farhana put on her *hijab* each morning with a sense of gratitude: so far, things had been so easy. She was able to keep her fast, pray all her prayers more or less on time, keep out of the vicious gossip circles she had once been a part of and maintain her high grades.

She spoke to Auntie Najma every night and was encouraged by her enthusiasm at her progress.

And she began to feel different. Ramadan was no longer just a month of fasting. She felt as if she was growing stronger all the time, more spiritually aware, becoming a *real* Muslim.

Faraz felt it too. He had been praying on time, letting his stubble grow a few more inches, listening to *Qur'an* on his iPod.

The long nights of standing in prayer affected him in the day. Yes, he was tired, but he was also more at peace, less desperate to prove himself. His confidence grew and, thankfully, the rest of the school seemed to calm down too. There were fewer confrontations between the boys, there was less beef. Even Maj seemed to melt into the background.

Faraz was grateful for that. He didn't need Maj and his lot getting him off track. Strangely enough, he hadn't heard from Skrooz in a while, either. It was probably just as well. Skrooz was like a relic from a past life now, a different reality, one he didn't want to have to face again.

For now, it was easier to believe that everything would be all right. That he could stay high on *iman*, on faith, and keep getting stronger every day.

Chapter 12

Temptation

Funny how things can change. Sometimes, all it takes is a phone call.

"Fraz! Where you been, man?"

Faraz instantly recognised the thick voice on the other end of the phone and his mouth went dry. Skrooz.

"Hey, Skrooz." He tried to sound casual. "Where have *you* been? Haven't heard from you in ages…"

"I had to go down London for a bit, y'know, keep a low profile. But it's safe now, I'm back. We need to hook up, man."

No, we don't, thought Faraz. *That's the last thing I need…*

"You seen any of the other lads while I've been away?"

"Uhh, I've been keeping my head down, y'know..."

"Nah, that's safe, that's safe. Anyway, I'm back now so you can come and hang with us again. We've still got to get you sorted, innit?"

"Sorted?"

"You know, make you *official* and everything. You're still down to be part of the crew, right?"

"Yeah, that's right..." said Faraz miserably. How was he going to get this guy off his case? He took a deep breath. "Only thing is, Skrooz, I've got quite a lot on at the moment, y'know? D'you think we could hook up in like, a few weeks' time?"

There was a long, cold silence. Then Skrooz's smooth voice with the sharp edge to it. "When Skrooz calls, you answer, blud. You know that. That's how it works. You're either in or you're out. And I know you don't want to be out... right?"

For the second time, Faraz found himself telling a lie. "Yeah, of course..."

"Safe. So I'll pick you up tomorrow after school? Got some stuff to take care of today..."

"OK."

"See you later then."

Faraz clicked the phone off. He had never despised himself more than in that moment. *What the hell do you think you're doing?*

But his internal monologue was broken by a painful shove in the back. Taken by surprise, he lurched forward, his hands flying out in front of him just in time to stop his face smacking into the tarmac. His phone clattered to the ground.

"We've got some unfinished business, you and me!" It was Maj.

Faraz's heart filled with dread and he began to feel sick. But he could not let Maj see he was afraid.

In an instant he was back on his feet.

You're fasting! You can't fight this guy now! The thought flashed through his mind, quicker than lightning, just as fleeting. It wasn't allowed to fight during Ramadan, the sacred month, not even getting angry was OK. But he couldn't back down now.

He squared up to Maj.

"What's your problem, man?" he shouted, his voice thick.

Maj was pushing him with both hands, the insults coming thick and fast.

Faraz felt the blood rush to his head as he pushed back, hard, pushing Maj's hands off his chest.

But Maj was at an advantage. Faraz had been standing near a wall and now he found himself backed up against it, trying to fend off Maj's blows.

The bell rang and a teacher's voice rang out across the courtyard.

"Hey! What's going on over there?"

Maj gave Faraz one last blow to the chest which left him winded, then turned to face the teacher who was making her way across towards them. He smiled at her, panting slightly.

"Nothing, Miss. Just messing around, that's all."

The teacher looked over at Faraz expectantly.

He forced himself to smile through the pain. "Sorry, Miss. Just messing about..."

She looked dubious. "Well, the bell's gone. You should both be in class. Off you go then!"

And the two boys nodded and hurried away, Faraz trying his best to walk steadily despite the pain in his chest and on his side.

The teacher watched them go. A waste of space,

some of these Asian lads were. Absolutely nothing going for them whatsoever.

It was only at home-time that Faraz realised Maj had taken his phone.

★ ★ ★

At home, he had to try to explain what had happened to his phone during *iftar*.

Farhana was appalled. "That school of yours is mad! Why did no one step in to stop it?"

Ammiji was worried too. They had chosen that school because it was close by and had a lot of Pakistani children in it. They couldn't really afford the fees for a Muslim school – an Asian majority school had to be just as good, they reasoned. But there were times when she doubted the wisdom of their decision.

Meanwhile, Dad laughed about the incident. "Boys will be boys, eh? Stop fussing over him, Uzma, you'll turn him into a mummy's boy!"

"But this is serious, *beta*. This boy has beaten up our son and taken his phone… I think we should do something."

"Ah, he has to learn to defend himself

sometime! Do you know how many fights I got into at school? You ask my mother, she'll tell you! By the time I was fifteen, no one could touch me – they were too afraid!"

Ammiji gritted her teeth. *Yes, but Faraz is not like you! Can't you see that?* But out loud she said, "So, what about the phone then?"

Dad scratched his head. "Well, the phone is a different matter. I will call the Head tomorrow. We'll get it back, don't worry."

Later, Farhana came to Faraz's room and caught him nursing his wounds. "Faraz, you OK?"

Faraz nodded, then rubbed his side and grimaced. "That Maj is such an idiot, man!" he growled. "He's always on my case! I'd love to fix him once and for all..."

"Yeah, he sounds like a nasty piece of work." Then she paused. "But Faraz, how come you didn't just walk away? You're meant to be fasting, remember? You're not supposed to get angry and that..."

"What was I supposed to do? Say, 'Sorry, *brother*, I'm fasting, can this wait until after Eid?' Get real, Farhana!" His face was flushed and he felt ashamed. He hadn't wanted to fight during

Ramadan either, but some people just wouldn't be put off.

"I know," said Farhana quietly. "I know it can be hard to keep control of your feelings. Sometimes they just get in the way of all your good intentions…."

★ ★ ★

Farhana had received a phone call too. Her phone had rung just after she got in from school. Undisclosed number. She had answered it.

Idiot. It was Malik.

"Farhana?" His voice was smooth, deep, just as she remembered it, and her heart skipped a beat.

"M-m-malik?" She didn't trust herself to speak.

"Farhana!" She could hear the smile in his voice, the relief. Misplaced. "Farhana, why haven't you been answering my calls? I've been going crazy here without you, I swear I miss you so much. Where have you been?"

Farhana had to take a few moments to steady herself as the world tilted. Wasn't this what she had been longing to hear? But not now, not in Ramadan, not now when she had just decided to make a go of things, now that she had made so much progress.

Not now… please, not now.

"Umm, Malik, this isn't really a good time… I have to go…"

"Farhana, wait! Please don't hang up! I need to see you…"

"No, Malik, I can't do this now. You don't understand… this isn't going to work. We can't be together, not like you want. I'm changing… I'm trying to change… and it just wouldn't work. Please. Please try and understand."

"Farhana, listen, whatever it is, we can work it out. I know we can. I want to be with you, just you. I-I-I love you… I love you."

Silence.

Heart beating.

Tears stinging.

Oh, what a test. What a painful test…

"Please don't call me any more, Malik. I can't do this, OK?"

She cut off the phone and stuffed it under her pillow.

It rang again, the phone's vibrations shooting through her fingers. She bit her lip and shook her head, tears springing to her eyes again. The phone stopped ringing after what seemed like an eternity.

She let out a ragged breath and brushed her tears away. *Just forget about it,* she told herself. *It doesn't matter. This is just a test. Allah will see you through.*

But he called again.

And again.

And again.

By the time she pushed the 'off' button on her phone, Farhana was sobbing, her hand over her mouth to stop the sound escaping. She couldn't take the pain, couldn't draw breath, couldn't stop the sobs that rose in her chest. Shaking, she curled over on to her right side and pulled the covers about her, over her shoulders, over her head, into her mouth. Anything to stop the sound escaping.

Chapter 13

First crack

Faraz was jittery when he got into school that morning. He hadn't slept well and had woken up too late to eat well at *sehri* time. He considered missing the fast that day, then swept the thought aside. That would be the first step down a slippery slope – that was what had happened last year. And, of course, he dreaded seeing Maj again. To make matters worse, Dad was sure to call the Head about his missing phone and he knew that was going to cause some trouble.

He certainly wasn't going to risk a fight with Maj and a possible detention or worse for the sake of a stupid phone. Besides, if he didn't get his phone back, it would be easier to avoid Skrooz.

As it was, the day passed without incident. Maj was nowhere to be seen, there was no message from the Head asking him to come to the office and

Faraz breathed a sigh of relief. Perhaps it would all be OK after all.

But at the end of the school day, as he walked out of the gates, he caught sight of Skrooz's car parked, waiting. It was hard to miss it. Skrooz and about four other lads were sitting on the black BMW, smoking, while music blasted out from the car's powerful speakers.

Skrooz spotted him and waved him over. Faraz could feel the other kids' eyes on him as he walked over to the sleek black car.

They envy me, the idiots, he thought.

"Hey, bro, good to see you – long time, eh?" Faraz found himself folded in Skrooz's embrace, inhaling smoke, cologne and sweat. He seemed even bigger than the last time he saw him.

Faraz greeted the other lads in turn. They all acknowledged him warily, the new favourite. He could see that they weren't that impressed with him.

What did Skrooz see in him, anyway? Was it his size? The fact that he looked like he could handle himself? Or did he sense a weakness in him, a desire to please, to be part of something?

Faraz dared not think about it as he got into the

car. *What are you doing, man?* But he was too afraid not to do what he knew they expected of him.

Everyone else piled in, Skrooz revved the engine several times, turned up the music and they were gone.

A crazy ride later, they parked up near an estate on the other side of town. He looked around at the others in the car through the smoke that hung, thick and cloying, in the close air of the car. Everyone was smoking something, everyone except him. He had never tried weed before. Being in the car, in that enclosed space, breathing in the slightly sweet smoky air was enough to make him feel light-headed.

His mind began to drift away from the guys' conversation about girls, guns and cars, stuff he wasn't really into anyway.

What are you doing here, Faraz? Is this what you want?

He knew that it wasn't, not now. Maybe a few weeks ago, he had wanted this more than anything in the world. But things were different now... how could he get out without getting burnt?

Then someone passed him a joint. Its end burned slowly, the smoke rising off it in a lazy stream, clear and distinct at first, then merging with the haze.

Faraz hesitated. *I'm fasting,* he thought to himself. *Say it.*

But he felt Skrooz's eyes on him. One look at his face and he knew that he would not be able to say anything.

Fumbling, he took the joint between his thumb and index finger, just like he had seen them do in the movies, as he had seen Skrooz do, and brought it to his lips.

He breathed in. The end glowed, red. He heard the crackle and hiss of burning paper.

The smoke hit his throat, harsh and fiery and tears sprang to his eyes. Try as he might, he couldn't contain the cough that erupted in his chest, his throat reacting furiously to the assault. He tried to hold in the smoke for as long as he could but eventually had to give up, hand the joint back, wheezing and spluttering.

The others roared with laughter, slapping him on the back, remembering their first time, ribbing him good-naturedly.

"It's always like that the first time," smiled Mo, one of the lads, taking a long, deep drag of the smouldering joint.

Faraz coughed and tried to laugh, tears streaming down his face. Whether from the heat of the joint or from shame, the tears came. He had broken his fast. He had cracked.

But the lads weren't laughing at him, they were laughing with him. They had all shared this ritual, this rite of passage, and now he was part of it too, whether he liked it or not.

Then Skrooz spoke. "What's up, Fraz? What's on your mind? You ain't been yourself…"

Faraz shook his head. "Nothing, man, nothing, just some beef at school…"

"Yeah?" Skrooz leaned over from the front seat. "Who's been troubling you, man?"

"This guy in my year, Maj, he started some trouble during one of my lessons. He said I wasn't nothing and that you wouldn't be able to help me there, at school… Then he took my phone…"

Skrooz's eyes clouded with anger.

"Nobody messes with the lads and gets away with it. Did you say his name was Maj?"

"Yeah." Faraz was afraid of the look in Skrooz's eyes: furious yet cold.

"Oi, that's the bloke from the other side

of the green," said Mo. "He rolls with dem lot from the Eastside Estate. Dem lot are trouble makers, man."

"Then I think it's time we taught them a lesson, don't you?" Skrooz looked around at the others in the car who all nodded gravely.

"Dem lot need to be taught some manners, learn how to have respect..."

"Dey ain't got no respect, man!"

"Sort them out, blud, that's what we have to do!"

Everyone in the car was angry now, fired up, ready to defend one of their own. Faraz saw the rage in their eyes and was glad that the rage was on his behalf and that he would not be on the receiving end – this time.

Just then, two girls came walking by the car, the shorter one pushing a young baby in a buggy. They were English, these girls, white girls from the estate, dressed in velour tracksuits, their hair slicked back from their faces, their large earrings almost identical.

They slowed down to look into the car and Skrooz saw them. His eyes lit up and he quickly stepped out of the car. "Hey, Natalie! How you doin', love?" he called out to the one walking with her hands in her pockets.

She turned to face him and snapped her gum, smiling at him, eyeing the car, his diamond rings.

"Yeah, I'm good... haven't seen you much around here. Where've you been?"

"Takin' care of business, that's all," was Skrooz's reply. "What you doin' now?"

"Going over to me nan's – me mam's not home..."

"Forget that, man, come for a ride with us... we'll have some fun."

The girl laughed then. "What kind of fun you have in mind, Skrooz?" She was teasing him.

"You know..." he said before ducking back into the car and grinning at the rest of the lads. "What do you say we have a bit of fun, lads?"

The others all nodded, grinning at the girl standing by the car door.

"What about the other one?" asked Mo, jerking his head towards the girl with the pushchair.

Skrooz shrugged his shoulders.

"What about your mate? Does she want to come along too?"

Natalie glanced over at her friend, who gave her a look and pointed to the buggy.

"Just drop him at home," Natalie hissed. "Come on, we'll wait for you."

Her friend stomped off, the buggy's wheels rattling against the rough pavement.

It was only when the girl got into the front seat and lit up a cigarette that Faraz saw how young she really was - she couldn't have been more than fourteen, fifteen at the most.

Everything felt so wrong. He looked out of the window, at the tattered grey estate, suddenly feeling alone and lost, as if the path in front of him had gone murky all of a sudden.

The others were hyped up, he could feel it in the air, and when the other girl walked up to the car without her child, they all cheered and passed around a fresh joint. The girls had several drags too. They weren't amateurs, clearly.

Faraz felt the air close round him again. He had to get out of there. He tapped Skrooz on the shoulder as he revved the car again and again, his hand on Natalie's thigh.

"I think I'll get home early, if that's all right." He had to shout over the noise of the engine, the music blasting from the speakers and the loud conversation all around him.

Skrooz looked at him closely, his eyes narrowed.

What is he looking for? What does he see?

But then his face relaxed into a smile and he nodded. "No problem, bro, no problem. We'll drop you, OK?"

"Nah, don't bother, I'll take the bus."

"It's far, y'know…"

"Yeah, I know, but I've got some things I need to take care of anyway."

Skrooz nodded and said, "OK, then, d'you want a ride to school tomorrow?"

"Yeah," replied Faraz, opening the car door, dragging his schoolbag out from beneath the seat. "That would be great. See you, guys."

He raised his hand to wave at them but they had already revved off down the street. The sound of the girls' playful screams echoed in his ears.

It took Faraz over two hours to get home. He got lost once and fell asleep, missing his stop. When he got off the bus he was sick on the grass verge.

He had seen the men coming home from the mosque. He had missed the *tarawih* prayers for the first time.

When he got in, the house was dark. He let himself into the house and was about to go upstairs when he saw that the lamp in the living room was on. Was someone still up?

He looked into the room and saw Farhana lying on the couch, asleep, a book lying on the floor by her hand. Her mobile phone lay face down. He picked it up and looked at the screen. Seven missed calls from someone called 'M' in her phonebook. He shrugged and put it down again.

Faraz looked over at his sister's sleeping face and his heart softened. She had waited up for him. And once again, he was overcome with shame, thinking of where he had been, who he had been with, what he had been doing.

There was a cashmere throw draped over the back of the sofa. Faraz picked it up, shook it out and, ever so gently, laid it over his sister, pulling it up to her neck. When the soft fabric brushed her face, she stirred and her eyes fluttered open.

"Faraz..?" Her voice was husky with sleep.

"I'm here, sis," he whispered.

"What time is it?" Farhana sat up, looking at her watch, rubbing the sleep out of her eyes. "Where have you been? You look terrible…"

"Just went for a ride with the lads, that's all."

Farhana sighed. "Oh? I thought you had gone to pray *tarawih*…"

"Yeah, I kind of missed it… listen, sis, I'm knackered. Gotta get to bed now." He got up to leave but she reached out and grabbed his hand.

"Faraz…" she said. "Are you OK?"

He squeezed her hand and fought to hold back tears. He didn't want her to worry. "I'll be all right, sis, don't worry."

"Insha Allah, Faraz, *insha Allah."*

Insha Allah, he said to himself. *I'll be all right.*

Chapter 14

Crime and punishment

Ammiji was still upset about Farhana's *hijab*.
She grew agitated every time she saw her with it on
and took every opportunity to criticise or ridicule
it: it was too big, too wide, like an old woman's,
it didn't suit her, made her look washed-out, made
her look ugly. Ammiji was suddenly concerned
with Farhana's education and career: the *hijab*
would limit her opportunities, would affect her
grades, make job-hunting harder, make her a social
outcast.

At first Farhana tried reasoning with her.
"But, Ammiji," she said, "the women during the
time of the Prophet Muhammad wore scarves.
Allah tells the believing women to cover in the
Qur'an..."

"To be *modest*, Farhana, to be modest!" was her

mother's reply. "There is a difference."

"But all his female relations wore it, and all the female companions –"

But Ammiji refused to consider Farhana's arguments.

"My mother used to recite *Qur'an* every day, Farhana, she was well-known for her generosity, and she never wore *hijab*. Are you saying that she was a bad person? That your Naneeji is a bad person? That I am a bad person?"

"Ammiji, this has nothing to do with you or Naneeji, or anyone else! This is between me and Allah. Please try and understand that. I am not judging anyone…"

"Of course you are!" retorted her mum. "You are saying that you are right and we are wrong. That you are a better Muslim than we are, those who have lived longer in this world and know more than you!"

Farhana gave up then.

★ ★ ★

This tension made Farhana hesitant to ask her mum about going out to *iftar* with her aunt.

As it happened, when she did finally pluck up the courage to ask, her mum had already made other plans.

"No, Farhana," had been her answer. "We are busy this weekend. Uncle Munir is coming over for *iftar* with his family and I need your help here to prepare the meal."

"But Ammiji, Auntie Najma invited me and I would really like to go. I haven't really been anywhere for *iftar* so far this year, apart from Naneeji's house…"

"Well I'm sorry, Farhana, but there's a lot to do here. You know how busy it is during Ramzan. You'll just have to keep your socialising until after Eid…"

"What socialising? I never go anywhere anyway!" Farhana felt the heat rise to her cheeks and she struggled to keep the anger out of her voice. It wouldn't do to lose her temper now.

She took a deep breath and tried again. "Please, Ammiji? I'll help you prepare all the food before I go… it's just that we were going to pray *tarawih* after *iftar* at the mosque Auntie Najma goes to…"

Her mum spun round to face her and Farhana could see the anger in her eyes.

"Oh, so that's the plan, is it? You want to go out with Najma and her crazy friends? Well, you can forget it! The less you see of those types of people, the better. It's bad enough you have to wear that thing on your head – next you'll be talking about *abayah*, *jilbab*, *niqab*, criticising how we do things and wanting to marry some fanatic with a big beard! I'm not having you coming home brainwashed and full of crazy ideas. You can just forget it."

Farhana could hardly believe her ears. She knew that her mum and Auntie Najma had their differences but this? Her mum was still talking, ranting about Najma and her extremist ideas.

Farhana knew better than to speak just then, so she simply looked down at the floor until her mum had finished.

★ ★ ★

So Auntie Najma didn't come to the *iftar* that Friday, when Uncle Munir and his family came over. Farhana had to excuse herself from a debate team meeting to get home to help her mum prepare.

The meal was delicious, as usual. Farhana was particularly proud of the *roti* as she had made it all by herself. It went beautifully with her mum's lamb curry and everyone was full of compliments.

"Hmm, we shall have to tell Sajid, eh?" Uncle Munir had laughed, winking at Farhana's mum. "You are training her well, Uzma!"

Mum had merely smiled demurely.

After *iftar*, the men got ready to go to the mosque to pray *isha* and then *tarawih*. Farhana gazed at them enviously. Once again, she would not be going but, even worse, she knew that Auntie Najma was going to be at her mosque, praying that night. Her heart ached to join her.

She tried to busy herself with the tidying up and decided that, as soon as she could get away, she would go and pray upstairs in her room. It was better than nothing, after all.

When she had finished clearing up the kitchen, Farhana made her way to the living room to say goodnight to everyone. She stopped short at the door. The room was bristling with tension.

"I won't allow it!" Naneeji was saying, shaking her head adamantly.

"But what can you do, Ammiji," pleaded Auntie Sajda, "if that's what she wants…"

"What she wants?" Naneeji spat out. "Since

when was getting married about 'what you want'? It's a disgrace, a complete disgrace! A girl's actions reflect on the whole family – she carries the *izzat*, the pride and honour, of the whole family. That is more important than what she wants!

"That's the trouble with living in this country," continued Naneeji hoarsely. "Our children get all sorts of funny ideas and they expect us to just go along with it – well I won't!"

"And you shouldn't have to, Ammiji," soothed Auntie Anisa, squeezing her mother's hand. "It's so unfair for her to do this to you, especially now…"

Auntie Sajda glared at them both. "Why are we sitting here talking about *izzat*? We're talking about our sister's life, about her choices, about her happiness! And anyway, what about Nabeel, our cousin? I don't remember you being too keen on marrying him!"

Auntie Anisa bit her lip and glanced at her mother, whose face darkened at the memory of that difficult time. It had taken a long time for her sister and the rest of the family in Pakistan to forgive her for that one.

"Why did you have to bring that up now, Sajda?

That was over twenty years ago…"

"To prove my point! You wouldn't marry your cousin, any more than Najma will marry some guy just because he's Pakistani and has the right job!"

"But a *gora*, Sajda? A *gora*? A white man? How can I allow that? How?" Naneeji's face crumpled and tears began to course down her face. The thought of one of her children marrying a non-Pakistani, a white man, filled her with shame and she buried her face in her *dupatta* and wept.

"But at least he's Muslim, Ammiji, that's something, isn't it? There are loads of Asian girls marrying English men, non-Muslims even, these days! Be thankful Najma isn't looking for that!"

"What difference will that make? What will everyone think of us? Our daughter married to a *gora*, as if we couldn't find her a good Pakistani husband? The shame! The shame!"

So that was what it was all about. Farhana didn't come out of the shadow of the doorway. She was reeling with shock.

So, her auntie wanted to get married at last. The family had been discussing it for a long time. After all, this was something that concerned all of them: a Pakistani marriage, like all Muslim unions, was one between families, not just individuals.

There had been men who had asked after her, sons of friends of the family, cousins from Pakistan, eager to marry a university graduate who was still 'religious'. But when they realised just how religious she was, they soon changed their minds.

But there had been one, a hopeful one, that she had heard her mum and aunts mentioning. He ticked all the boxes: Pakistani, educated - a doctor in fact - fair skinned, from a good family, respectable.

The only trouble was Auntie Najma wasn't interested in those boxes. She was looking for more, something different.

"I'm not going to marry just anyone, you know," Auntie Najma had said in their last discussion about marriage. "I'm looking for someone who shares my passions, someone I can grow with, someone who will stretch and challenge me, always believing in me and supporting me in my dreams…"

"And you expect to find all this in a *desi*?" Farhana had asked sarcastically.

"To be honest, I don't care where he's from,"

had been her aunt's reply. "If he's a Muslim and has a good heart and wants me for *me*, for who I am, I'm game... and being drop-dead gorgeous wouldn't hurt either!"

Oh, Auntie Najma, you've done it again. Once a rebel, always a rebel, eh?

And Farhana felt a sneaking sense of pride in her aunt's fearlessness, even as her heart twisted to hear her mother and aunts argue so bitterly.

★ ★ ★

The men decided to come back to the house after *tarawih*. It had been a long time since they had all had time together and there were many issues to discuss. No sooner had they settled into the lounge than Faraz heard his new ring tone and jumped. Who would be calling him at this time? His father raised his eyebrows when he saw Faraz rush to answer his sleek new phone.

A gift from Skrooz.

"Here you go, Fraz," he had said, all casual like.

Faraz's eyes had widened as he recognised the latest model from all the billboard ads down the town centre. "Are you sure, bruv? I mean, I can pay you, if you want."

Skrooz had laughed then, showing his gold tooth.

"Nah, Fraz, there'll be plenty of time for that later. You be cool and enjoy the phone. You one of the lads, innit? All the lads have this model... ."

Faraz felt his heart swell with a mixture of shame and pride. Was he one of the lads? How could he be when every time he saw them, guilt gnawed at his insides and he felt as if he was betraying himself?

Sure enough, it was Skrooz on the phone. He sounded breathless, his voice husky.

"Fraz, man, you have to get down here!"

Faraz quickly stepped into the passage. He shook his head to try to clear his mind.

"Get down where, man?"

"We're heading for the Eastside Estate, going to teach that guy Maj a lesson. You have to be there."

"What, *now*?" His mind darted to the *tarawih* prayers he had just prayed, to his English homework waiting upstairs on his desk.

"Yes, Fraz," came the reply, as hard as steel. "Now. We'll be there to get you in ten minutes. Be ready."

The phone went dead, leaving Faraz standing in the hallway, mute, his hand wet with sweat where he held the phone.

"Faraz?" His head jerked up to see Farhana standing in the corridor, a pile of books in her arms. "Are you OK? You look terrible…"

She went to put the books down and come towards him but he waved her away, backing towards the stairs, away from the room where his father sat with his uncles and cousins, discussing the latest news from Pakistan and the situation in Palestine.

"I'm fine, sis, just fine… got to go out for a minute, that's all…"

"Faraz, what's up? What's happened?"

"Nothing, Farhana, don't worry." Faraz tried to make his voice normal again. "I just need to go and sort something out… let Ammiji know I've gone out, will you?"

"OK…" His sister frowned, still worried. "I don't understand, but… be careful, Faraz…"

Grateful to have avoided more questions, Faraz grabbed his coat and headed for the front door. He reached the pavement just as Skrooz's car pulled up. With just one quick furtive glance around him,

Faraz disappeared into the car.

From the kitchen window, Farhana watched, unseen. The moonlight shimmered on the tears that stood in her eyes.

The atmosphere in the car was tense, quite different from the other evening. Hardly anyone spoke. When they neared the Eastside Estate, Skrooz pulled up about two blocks away.

"They're at a party in that house over there..." He pointed to a small house on the edge of the estate, with a tatty front yard and a dull light glowing in the windows.

"They've been getting out of line, these lads. It's time we sorted them out, showed them who's in charge around here." He looked over at Faraz. "Do you want to handle Maj or should I sort him out?"

Faraz felt faint. What did he mean 'handle'? What did he expect him to do?

"Er, I'll take him," he said with as much conviction as he could muster.

"OK, then. Mo, get the stuff out of the trunk."

Obediently, Mo got out of the car and opened the trunk. After a few moments, he was back with his hands full. Baseball bats, heavy clubs and a couple of knives whose fierce blades glinted in the lamplight. Mo thrust a bat in Faraz's direction. Clearly, he could not be trusted with a knife just yet.

"So, we go in there and send them a message. Just a message, that's all. And Faraz will take Maj. Let's go"

Faraz felt light-headed as he walked, the middle of the huddle of lads, all tattoos and leather jackets, towards the front door.

As they got there, the front door opened and a girl spilled out, followed closely by an Asian lad in baggy jeans.

"Oi, come here, you!" he called after her, his speech slurred. She giggled and lurched across the yard, daring him to follow.

When she got to the gate, she looked up and screamed, a startled scream that seemed to claw at her throat. The Asian lad stopped short and struggled to focus. He lifted his face to the harsh glare of the streetlight.

It was Maj.

Through the fog of alcohol, he saw a group of guys, big guys, about six of them, all strangely familiar. They were all armed. The flash of the knife in the biggest one's hand brought him to his senses and he cursed loudly and tried to scramble back into the house.

"Get him!" roared Skrooz and the lads moved, like one body, flooding the garden in an instant.

As the girl in the yard screamed, all the guys rushed the door which Maj was desperately trying to close behind him. They could hear him yelling for his mates, trying to get their attention. But the music and laughter drowned his voice just enough for Faraz and the lads to push the door open. And then all hell broke loose.

The house became a seething mass of bodies: girls in party dresses flew this way and that, screaming, as Skrooz and the others strode into the living room, swinging their baseball bats, smashing bottles, tables, faces, anything that stood in their way.

Faraz was thrust into the room by the movement of the others. In a moment, Maj was in front of him, fear distorting his face. Something primordial took over inside Faraz. His mind flooded with images: the black rainbow that had ruined his picture, the slaps, the punches, the taunts, his phone.

As if in slow motion, he felt the weight of the bat in his hand.

He felt it catch the air as he swung it above his head.

The air whistled as he brought the bat down, down, down, towards Maj.

He heard the sickening thud as the wood made contact with flesh and bone.

He saw Maj crumple and collapse to the floor.

He heard the blood roar in his ears and felt his heart pound in his chest.

The whole room seemed to come to a standstill. Then Faraz felt himself being jerked away and shoved through the room, past the upturned sofas and broken bottles, towards the car. The others whooped with glee, shouting curses at the boys who were left in the house, assessing the damage.

Faraz found that he was shaking, shaking, as the adrenalin pumped its way out of his system. The others all congratulated him and he smiled shakily.

He didn't think Maj would be giving him any more trouble.

★ ★ ★

When he got home, even Farhana wasn't up waiting for him. He was completely alone as he took a shower and struggled to pray, to concentrate, to understand what was happening to him.

That night, he dreamt again of the strange alien city, of the road that began to slope upwards, upwards, until he was struggling to find footholds with his toes, fingers, anything.

His nails splintered and his fingertips bled as he began to slide down the rough tarmac, slowly at first, then faster and faster, his knees scraping the tar, his teeth jarring. Then darkness, the terrifying darkness began to close over him, shutting out the streetlights and the air around him. He began to struggle for breath.

Chapter 15

Payback time

Farhana tried hard to wake Faraz for the morning prayer but he was like a lump of lead. In the end, she had to leave him sleeping to avoid missing it altogether.

When he wandered down later, bleary-eyed, asking, "Did I miss *sehri*?" she was furious.

"Of course you missed it, Faraz! What time did you get in last night anyway? And where did you go?"

Faraz's head hurt and he waved away his sister's questions. "I was just out, OK?"

"With Skrooz?"

Faraz looked away then. "Yeah... we had some stuff to take care of."

"Stuff, Faraz? What *stuff*? And why have you gone back to hanging with those lads anyway?

I thought you were past all that... I thought things were going to be different..."

Faraz turned on Farhana, his face red with anger. "Well, maybe it's not that easy to be 'past that'! Listen, sis, spare me the lecture, OK? I can handle myself and I know what I'm doing. Just do yourself a favour and stay out of my business!"

"Stay out of your business...?" Farhana's voice faltered, her eyes clouding with confusion. It had been so long since they had had an argument, so long since they had raised their voices to each other, she wasn't used to it any more. And after the closeness they had shared this Ramadan, it seemed so strange. And it hurt. It hurt to be pushed away.

She blinked back tears. "All right," she said then, quietly, "I will." And she left the room. She had a presentation to prepare for.

Faraz let out a ragged breath and nursed his anger. What did she know about what he was going through? What gave her the right to judge? She had the perfect life, always had done. There was no way she would understand his situation. Farhana was the kind of person who would tell you to shove off to your face, would defend her corner, stand up for what she knew to be right. He had never had that kind of courage.

And now his inability to stand up for himself was taking him down a road he had never travelled before, one where he felt compelled to do things, say things, that were as far from his true nature as they could be.

But how am I going to get myself out of this? How?

The question plagued him every moment of that day. And he got a detention for not having done his English homework.

★ ★ ★

"Right, Fraz," said Skrooz that night. "It's time you started doing your bit for the collective."

They were sitting in Skrooz's smoke-filled car on a quiet side street.

"To be part of the crew, you have to earn your keep, see? It's simple: you help me, I help you, we all benefit. Cos there is only one language that we speak around here, only one language everyone understands. That language is money. Money is power. And if you control the money – who makes it, who takes it, who spends it – you control everything.

"Dem idiots like Maj think that they can have a piece but they don't know. We ain't interested in no power-sharing. It's either we run things, or we destroy dem. Personally, I ain't interested in destroying nothin', cos it's all sweet right now. And you're gonna help keep it that way, see?"

He brought out five plastic packets, hardly bigger than his hand. Two brown, three white. Heroin and cocaine, they had to be.

"I want you to carry these, take them to this address..."

Faraz's eyes opened wide and his heart fluttered. What was he asking him to do? Carry bags of illegal drugs?

"The police are getting a bit cheeky around here. They keep wantin' to stop and search me, thinkin' I'm up to illegal dealings. But the thing is, yeah, I'm clean. They will never find anything on me. Why? Cos I got clean, pretty boys like you to do my dirty work for me. And then when the money comes in, you get a piece, simple as that."

Faraz's eyes darkened and he looked around fearfully. All the other lads were staring at him, their eyes fixed on his face, looking for a reaction.

"No!" he screamed inside and his mouth opened, then shut again.

"Good lad," smirked Skrooz. "If you're cool, I'm cool, yeah? You know what *izzat* means, right Fraz? Your honour, your reputation. Well, dis is your *izzat*, right here, bro: the *izzat* of the streets."

Then Skrooz leaned in, so close that Faraz could smell his smoke-tinged breath and see the red lines on his eyeballs, the open pores on his nose, every thick hair that formed his eyebrows.

"And know dis, Fraz," he said softly. "No one crosses me, y'hear? No one. If I call you, you answer. If I send you, you go. If I want you, you come. Cos if you don't, I can make you pay in ways you could never imagine." Then he sat back in his seat and proceeded to light a cigarette. "But we don't even have to talk about that now, do we..."

Faraz swallowed hard, his heart hammering in his chest, his throat dry. He shook his head. No, they didn't have to talk about that.

★ ★ ★

The next two weeks were like a patchwork of horrors for Faraz. Every time his new mobile phone rang, his heart sank. So far, only his family and Skrooz had this number, and since his father hardly ever rang him on the mobile and he and Farhana had not yet made up, it was usually Skrooz calling to tell him to meet him after school.

After getting into the smoke-filled BMW, there was no telling what would go down: teaching some lads a lesson, dropping off some stolen goods, picking up a stash of weed, dropping off the brown and white packets, sometimes with another member of the crew, sometimes on his own. And money, money, money. There was always so much money, to be paid, to be collected, to be spent.

At first, Faraz's conscience tore at him. His heart ached every time he missed the pre-dawn meal, every time he noticed that it was sunset and realised that he hadn't prayed, not even once. Many times, while out with the lads, he would ache for the feeling of peaceful elation he had found during the *tarawih* prayers but, when he reached for it, it seemed beyond his grasp.

Not only that, but he was also acutely aware of the number of forbidden things, *haram*, even illegal things he was witness to. But even these things began to feel normal as he became used to living in Skrooz's world.

Whatever had sustained him at the beginning of Ramadan had all but seeped away, almost without him noticing. He had lost count of the number of times he had broken his fast.

His initial disgust with himself gave way to resignation. After all, this was reality he was dealing with right here, not some spiritual utopia. Besides, since their encounter with Maj and his gang, his reputation at school had received a huge boost. The story of how Fraz the Wrecker and Skrooz's crew had stormed the party became legendary, particularly since Maj sported an ugly scar on his forehead as proof for anyone who didn't believe the story.

For the most part, Maj lay low and kept his head down, admitting defeat. But more than once Faraz had caught him looking at him, hate burning in his eyes. It was almost as if he was biding his time.

★ ★ ★

One day, they finished their business early and Skrooz was in a good mood. There was still an hour of sunlight left when Skrooz suggested they go to the park. "I ain't been to the park in ages, man!"

They did look slightly out of place: a gang of big Asian lads in black hoodies and crew cuts walking past the mums in the playground with their children. They walked to the far side of the park. Although it backed on to an estate, it was quiet here; there was hardly anyone around.

"Us Pakis are funny, innit?" Skrooz said suddenly, taking a drag of his cigarette. "Y'see, our grandparents came to this country and worked hard to set up their little businesses and told their kids to study to become doctors and accountants. So our parents did all the studying, played by the rules and tried to get on in this society. But they thought they could win the game – they didn't realise that they would never be accepted, would never fit in.

"This society's racist, man, racist to the core. Even if they got a couple of coconut Pakis in government, it don't mean nothing. They hate us and they want to keep up down in every way they can: throwing us out of school, locking us up, setting up anti-terror laws and all those sorry excuses to harass us even more. But they don't know that lads like us, we don't want a piece of their bloody Middle England. We don't want their City jobs and poxy universities.

"We make it so that they are pissing themselves about our neighbourhoods, so scared they can't even come here cos *we* rule. This is our turf and there ain't a damn thing they can do about it..." He sucked hard on his cigarette, looking over at the playground.

"Me mam used to bring me here," he said then, almost to himself. "She don't understand though. She still wishes I had become an engineer or doctor or some crap like that. I tell you, when she gets on my case about getting a job, I just leave some money on the table. She don't ask where it come from and I don't tell her. No need for her to be knowin' dem tings."

"What about your dad?" Faraz wanted to know.

"Nah, man, my dad divorced my mum when I was a kid. I'm the man of the house now and she knows it. She don't ask me what I get up to as long as I put money on the table and keep my brothers and sisters in check."

"What d'you mean?"

The look on Skrooz's face made Faraz think he shouldn't have asked. But he continued anyway. He was clearly in the mood to talk.

"Dem kids are too wild, innit. They don't show no respect to my mum so it's up to me to sort them out. Give them a few slaps if they get out of line. Take my sister, yeah? She's eighteen, right, thinks she knows it all. Till I find out she's seeing some guy. Well, we sorted him out good and proper, didn't we, lads?"

The rest of the group cheered and thumped Skrooz on the back.

He took a sip from his can then spat into the grass. "Think he can mess with my sister... chief!"

"Nah, man," added Imti, another of the lads. "That is the ultimate in disrespect, for mans to be messin' with my sisters. Can't allow dat to happen, no way."

There was general agreement. Just then, they saw Natalie and her friend walking on the path into the park with their buggy. They had come through from the estate behind them. Natalie smiled and waved. Skrooz kissed his teeth and turned away. "I don't like cheap hos, man," he muttered through clenched teeth.

Faraz said nothing. Skrooz and his friends had seemed to like them well enough a few weeks ago.

Natalie's wide smile vanished when she saw that she wasn't welcome and she flicked her ponytail and walked on.

After a short period of silence Skrooz continued. "You see, that's why I'll only ever marry one of our girls. The rest of them are just nasty. Cos if you're gonna marry someone you need to know that they ain't been anywhere, that they ain't been with no one else."

"That's right!" said Mo fiercely. "I ain't never gettin' played by one of these biaitches here! I love my money too much!"

They all burst out laughing. Mo was known as the stingiest out of all of them.

Faraz laughed too but with a sense of bewilderment. The irony of the conversation was not lost on him.

Chapter 16

Doubt and betrayal

Farhana was falling too although she wouldn't admit it. She had managed to keep fasting, but only just. Her prayers had become a series of movements, hurried and shallow. She found it hard to pour herself into anything vaguely religious. Her arguments with her mum were wearing her down and worry about Faraz gnawed at her constantly.

"I'm really worried about him, Auntie," she had confided in Auntie Najma the day before. "He's started hanging with these guys again and they're no good, I know it."

"Yeah," agreed Auntie Najma, "he was kind of evasive the last few times I spoke to him. Has he had any more contact with those brothers from the arts organisation?"

"Oh, that? He hasn't mentioned it at all. It's like he's totally clammed up – won't speak to me about anything now."

"Hmmm, I will have to get down there soon..."

"Well, I would keep a safe distance if I were you. You're not Ammiji's favourite person right now."

"She's still having trouble accepting your *hijab* then?"

"Oh yes. And as far as she is concerned, it's all your fault. So she's basically told me to stay away..."

"You mean you're not allowed to see me?"

"Well, basically, yeah. If she knows that you've invited me somewhere or that you're going to be at a certain place, all of a sudden, we're too busy, we can't go... it's crazy. And now with this *gora* situation..."

"Oh, yes, there's that." Then Auntie Najma's voice changed. "Listen, I don't want you worrying about that, OK? It's all in Allah's hands so don't stress yourself. Just remember to keep focused. Keep worshipping Allah, keep respecting your mum and don't upset her on my account. We'll find another way around it, *insha Allah*...Got to run now, honey, and get back to work."

"Oh, Auntie?"

"Yes, honey?"

"Umm… nothing, it's OK…"

"You sure?"

"Yeah, it's fine. It's fine…."

★ ★ ★

But it wasn't fine.

Farhana's *hijab* felt heavy now, heavier than it had ever been. Heavier than when her mum questioned her about it, making her feel as if she had done the wrong thing, that she was on her way to becoming an 'extremist'. Heavier than when she found that she was no longer the centre of attention at school. Heavier than when, after the initial honeymoon period when her wearing the *hijab* was a novelty and a number of the girls had admired her brave decision, the hype moved elsewhere.

It was strange. When she had first put on the *hijab*, she had felt strong, powerful, in control. She was pleased when guys hardly gave her a second glance. She enjoyed the fact that they didn't call out after her, asking for her number, complimenting her on her hair, her eyes, or whatever they thought she wanted to hear.

Now they averted their eyes or mumbled their greetings. That was how they had been brought up – this was how their mothers dressed, after all.

So this is what it feels like to be respected, Farhana had thought to herself, and she was flooded with gratitude that she had been strong enough to do this.

But lately, she had lost some of that confidence, that immunity to guys' indifference to her. It had started to bother her that their eyes glazed over when they saw her, sliding away from her face, brightening when they saw Robina's cheeky smile and highlighted hair.

Her pride was hurt, her vanity bristled: everyone knew she was ten times prettier than Robina!

Once upon a time, she had been the darling of every clique that mattered. Now, in her *hijab*, she was considered a pariah, especially as she hadn't gone the 'hijabi fashionista' route. Some girls she knew wore a scarf but teamed it with the latest skinny jeans or skirts with knee-high boots, chunky accessories and expertly applied make-up. And although she didn't want to wear her *hijab* that way, she couldn't help a stab of envy as she watched these 'trendy hijabis' strut their stuff.

"They have a name for them in the States, y'know," said Shazia when she caught Farhana looking at a group of girls make their giddy way to the bus stop.

"Ho-jabis," Shazia went on, trying to keep her lips from twitching.

"What?" Farhana was shocked. "You can't be serious! That is so wrong!" She looked at one of the girls adjusting the wide belt that cinched her waist as she clip clopped in her high street heels. "But then again..." She and Shazia burst out laughing.

"Well, at least they're trying, right?"

"Yeah, true, but my dad reckons that doesn't even count as *hijab* anyway," said Shazia. "Just because your head's covered don't mean you're dressed decently."

"But would your dad rather they didn't cover their heads at all?"

"Well, I've tried asking him that but he just says that in Islam, you need to submit totally, not half-heartedly."

"Your dad's really got a way of making you feel low, hasn't he? Like you can never be a good enough Muslim."

"Hmmm, not really," replied Shazia. "He is an *imam* after all, so he's studied the *Qur'an* and he knows a whole lot more than most people. It's just that he didn't grow up here. He doesn't know what it's like to grow up in a society where everything is calling out to you, offering you forbidden things. He sees everything in black and white and, you know what? Although I know that he's right most of the time, I just wish he would see things from my point of view once in a while and realise that it's not that easy to do what you know to be right."

"What about your mum? Does she talk to him about it?"

Shazia laughed. "My mum is constantly on at him! 'Junaid!' she says, 'you don't understand what it is like for young people these days!' He just smiles at me and says, 'Islam doesn't change, *beta*. You just have to be strong.' Then he'll give me a hug and I'll get all teary because I want to be what he expects of me – it's just so hard!"

"I guess I knew that *hijab* was a full-time

commitment – I guess I didn't think it would be so difficult..."

"You finding it hard?" asked Shazia softly.

Farhana took a deep breath. This was not familiar territory. Usually, it was Shazia who shared *her* fears and insecurities, Farhana who offered advice and comfort.

"I miss him, you know," she said quietly.

"Who, Malik?"

Farhana nodded. "It's like there's a little voice telling me that, if I wasn't wearing *hijab*, I'd be with him now..."

"But hold on, Farhana, *hijab* wasn't the reason you broke up with him, remember?"

Farhana's mind flashed back to that dreadful morning when Robina had rushed in to the classroom, full of the latest news, full of the story about Malik and that model.

Tears stung her eyes. "Yeah, I suppose you're right... I guess he just isn't who I thought he was, who he told me he was..."

Both girls were silent for a while. Then Shazia spoke.

"But Farhana, how come you're feeling this way? I always thought you were strong, too strong to let something like this phase you. You know what you're like: once you make up your mind about something, that's it, there's no shifting you."

"I know, Shaz, I know, that's why I'm finding it hard to understand what's going on with me at the moment. I just feel so weak, like everything is wearing me down. I don't know how long I can hold on…"

Shazia hugged her friend.

"Sounds like your *iman* is low. Have you spoken to your Auntie Naj about it?"

"You know what, Shaz, I haven't really spoken to her about the *hijab* - and Malik. She's going through her own stuff right now with the family…"

"So, is she still going to marry that white guy, then?"

"I honestly don't know. My granny is dead set against it but I think my eldest uncle, who is acting as Auntie Naj's *wali*, might be coming round to the idea…"

"Really?" Shazia's eyes were wide. "I wouldn't have expected that! He always seemed so stern to me…"

"Yeah, but my auntie is his baby sister and

we all know he has a soft spot for her. Besides, he will listen to the Islamic side of things more than Naneeji. Auntie Naj's argument is that, as long as he is a good Muslim, and he's a good person – respectable, responsible and all that – it shouldn't matter that he's not Pakistani. But Naneeji's more interested in culture and what 'the community' will say."

"Sounds familiar," murmured Shazia, thinking of her own grandmother. "But is all the aggro worth it? What if they don't accept him? What then?"

"Honestly, Shaz," sighed Farhana, "I just don't know."

"And what about the kids? How will they fit in? They won't be full Pakistani and white people will never accept them: they'll just be stuck in the middle. And what if it doesn't work out? Honestly, sometimes I think it's just not worth marrying out, rebelling like that, it's just easier to go with the flow. The family always wins in the end anyway…"

"Do you really believe that, Shaz?" Farhana didn't know what to think.

"Well, would you sacrifice your parents and the rest of your family for some guy you hardly know – because it's not like she's known him for ages. He's her friend's brother, they work at the same organisation and they've spoken a few times, that's it! At the end of the day, your family wants what's best for you..."

"What they *think* is best for you," interjected Farhana, "there's a difference. Auntie Naj says that he's strong in his *deen* and that she's seen a lot of his character through working with him. Plus, he's a revert so he understands the life that she's come from, what it was like living in London, what it means to have grown up here.

My family would rather marry her off to someone traditional who wouldn't understand that she's different, that she wants different things. She doesn't want to get into a marriage where things will be just like they were in her mum's house, the same old traditions, the same attitudes. She wants a marriage where she can grow. And most of all, she wants Islam, pure and simple, not our cultural version of it."

Farhana sighed. "Well, that's what she says anyway..."

★ ★ ★

When Farhana thought back to the first days and weeks of Ramadan, she could hardly recognise herself. She had been strong then, unshakeable. Her faith kept her heart at ease and her head high. Now she yearned for the peace she had felt then, blissfully immersed in the *Qur'an*, the prayer, the fasting, the night prayers of *tarawih*.

Where had it all gone?

She knew that the telephone call from Malik had been the beginning. That was when she first felt her resolve weakening. And then there was the constant struggle with her mum over her *hijab*, the estrangement from Faraz. Things still weren't right between them. For a start, he hadn't stopped hanging out with Skrooz and Farhana could not forgive him for that.

Despite her prayers, her feelings for Malik had not disappeared. They tormented her, especially at night. She missed him, wanted nothing more than to call him, to speak to him, to hear his voice. More than once, she had called his number, only to hang up as soon as it started ringing. She had managed to resist answering the phone when he had called back.

"You can be such an idiot, you know that,

Farhana?" Robina said while they waited for the next lesson to start. "Do you know how many girls would kill for the chance to go out with Malik? And you had him – and let him go! And now that you're wearing *hijab*, he'll never want you!"

"Well, isn't that the whole point of *hijab*?" Shazia rolled her eyes and adjusted her glasses. She had really had enough of Robina's attitude. It was as if, now that Farhana was covering up, Robina thought it was her duty to take over as the most popular girl in school.

"Well, Shaz," Robina turned to Shazia, "I can understand someone like you wearing *hijab* … after all, you're not exactly supermodel material, are you?" She smiled sweetly. "But Farhana? Come on!"

Shazia's face burned as several girls around her tittered. She blinked hard to hold back the tears that threatened to spill over, and swallowed the lump in her throat.

Farhana was furious. "Robina!" she whispered fiercely, "why do you have to be such a first class cow?"

"Oh, now, don't you start getting all self-righteous with me just cos I told your little sidekick here some truths about herself! You know me, Farhana, I like it when people know their place. At the end of the day, we all know you only hang out with her because you feel sorry for her!"

You're fasting, don't rise to the bait!

But one look at Shazia's horrified face and Farhana knew she would have to speak.

"What a load of rubbish! How dare you say something that's blatantly untrue? I've known Shazia forever, she's my best friend. And let me tell you something," she leaned over Robina's desk until her face was inches away. "Shazia is ten times the friend you are. You've just become a carbon copy of your sister: fake and shallow!"

"Shallow, huh?" Robina studied her nails, unphased by Farhana's words. "That's not what Malik told me last night…"

A shocked murmur rippled through the classroom. Farhana stepped away from Robina, swaying slightly as if she had been slapped in the face.

"What..?" she croaked.

Robina narrowed her eyes. "You heard me."

"You little …" Shazia couldn't bring herself to say more. "How could you do that to Farhana?"

Farhana simply stared at Robina, unable to process what she was saying. Malik? And Robina? It just didn't make any sense... but then again, it made perfect sense.

Robina was enjoying her moment of triumph. "Come on," she said, "all's fair in love and war, right?" She looked around the class, her left eyebrow raised. "You didn't really think he would wait around for you, did you?"

Farhana could no longer control the tears and, with one last look at the smirk on Robina's face, she ran out of the room. By the time she got to the toilets and locked herself in a cubicle, she was sobbing, the smell of disinfectant sharp in her nostrils.

Shazia came to see if she was all right, but she pleaded with her to leave her alone.

"I'll be back in a minute, Shaz, please..."

When her sobs had subsided, she came out of the cubicle and went to wash her face. She looked up at the pale face and the red eyes that stared back at her. She raised her hands to her head and pushed the white scarf back until it hung around her neck and several strands of her glossy hair fell forward. With her hands still on her shoulders, she began to cry again, looking at her reflection.

Where did I go wrong? Where?

* * *

Farhana went straight home after school and went upstairs to lie down. What was meant to be a short nap turned into a three hour sleep. When Farhana woke up, her room was dim and she could hear her mum calling her to come and break fast. She felt better after saying her prayers, stronger.

It was nice to see Faraz home for a change. She found herself looking at him often during the meal, trying to read his facial expressions, his silence.

After the family had eaten their *iftar*, Dad said, "Right, you two, your mother and I are going over to Uncle Ali's for a family meeting."

"What about, Dad?" asked Faraz.

Their dad glanced over at their mum who pressed her lips together and said nothing.

"It's about Auntie Naj, isn't it?" asked Farhana. "About her wanting to marry a *gora*, right?"

"Farhana," snapped her mother, "stay out of this! It has nothing to do with you! The family will decide what should be done about all this."

Faraz looked at Farhana. "You mean Auntie wants to marry someone who isn't Pakistani?"

Farhana nodded. "A white guy, Muslim though. Sounds like a really great guy, to be honest, and I think…"

"Farhana!" cried her mother. "How can you say that? You know how I feel about inter-racial marriages! They never work! What is so wrong about sticking to your own kind? Those who understand you best? Marrying out of your culture is a recipe for disaster…"

"My own kind?" Farhana's voice rose. "What do you mean, Ammiji? I was born in England! I grew up in England! I can barely speak Urdu! Why should I have more in common with a Pakistani from back home than someone born and raised here? How does that make any sense?"

"Farhana," growled her father, a warning in his voice. "You must respect your mother…"

"I do respect you, Ammiji – but that doesn't mean that I can't have my own opinion. Why do you expect us to be exactly like you? We're British, Ammiji, British Asian, British Muslim, whatever! We will never go back to the way we would have been if we had stayed in Pakistan. Would you rather Auntie Naj marries someone who may have different goals from her, who may not understand her, who can't make her happy, just because he is Pakistani?"

Mum tried to reply but Farhana kept talking. "I thought Islam was supposed to be inclusive. Does Allah look at our lineage or at our hearts? Let's face it, a lot of Asians don't want their children marrying out because they are racist, pure and simple!"

Farhana's father stared at her. "Now you are calling us racists, Farhana? Have you forgotten that it was our shop that was looted by those white thugs? That we are the ones being discriminated against every day?"

Farhana smiled sadly at her father. "It doesn't stop us judging people by their colour though, does it, Dad? Remember that girl I used to play with at school, Edith? The only reason you never invited her here was because she was black. And the only reason you are all so upset about Auntie Naj's choice is because he is white. I don't know what you call that, Ammiji, but I call it racism."

"I agree with Farhana, Mum," said Faraz, quietly.

His mum turned to stare at him, shocked. "Faraz!"

"But I do, Mum. It's not right to judge people like that... it's not right." He lowered his eyes and looked sideways at his sister who shot him a grateful look.

Both parents stared at their two children as if they could hardly recognise them. They both looked the same as they had always done, but also different somehow.

Ammiji noticed for the first time the dark circles under Farhana's eyes, her son's sallow skin. What had happened to her babies? She wanted to grab them both and hold them to her, like she had done when they were little. There had been no struggle then, no Pakistani or British, just a mother's love for her children. When was the last time she had hugged them?

But even as she looked at them, she felt a chasm of incomprehension widen between them, of truths untold, of secrets and defences and it scared her. She turned abruptly to the twins' father.

"We'd better go, *jaan*, or we'll be late." She got up, took another long look at both her children and left to go and wait in the car.

Dad looked over at Farhana and shook his head. "Well, *beta*, I don't know what to say…" he murmured.

"Say that you'll all give him a chance, Dad," said Farhana quietly. "He deserves that at least.…"

Chapter 17

Breaking point

The bell rang and Faraz left the art room, deep in thought. He had just completed a piece of Arabic calligraphy, graffiti style, and it was already up on the display board. Everyone had been well impressed.

"Where did you get the inspiration for this piece, Faraz?" Mr McCarthy's soft voice was full of admiration.

And Faraz told him about Ahmed Ali, the one-time illegal graffiti artist turned respected Muslim artistic figure.

"That sounds fantastic, Faraz!"

"Oh, it is, Sir. Just go down the town centre – you'll see his latest mural there. He invited me to come and do a wall with him, near the end of Ramadan…"

"Isn't that in a couple of weeks' time?"

Faraz nodded, shocked at how Ramadan was almost over. Where had his Ramadan gone? It was the last ten days already, the best days according to Islamic tradition.

He thought about the dream he had had the night before, the dream where the road was getting steeper and steeper and he was struggling to get a foothold. And then the darkness overtaking him. This time, the dream had continued.

When all was black, he realised that he couldn't breathe! He struggled against it at first but then he was in a shroud, a white shroud, and the air was suddenly filled with incense, and far away chanting. His eyes began to close as the life began to seep out of his body. And the last thing he saw was her face, Farhana's face...but it was fading, fading away... No! He had to stay, he had to! But it was too late.

All the lights went out and there was silence, just silence.

He had woken with a start, gasping for air, his hand on his chest, his pillow soaked with sweat. He'd sat there for a few moments, panting, willing his heart to beat again, the air to reach his lungs, the blood to flow through his veins, warm and alive.

Then he had glimpsed the first light of dawn above the rooftops. He might just make it.

He had kicked off his duvet and got out of bed, shaking with the effort. He'd made his way in the dark to the bathroom and made *wudhu*, washing his hands, nose, mouth, arms, face, head and feet. As the cold water touched his skin, he'd felt calm return to his body.

Wash it away, just wash it all away...if I'm breathing, it isn't too late...

Then he had taken down his prayer mat from his wardrobe where his mum always put it when she tidied up. Laying it out on the floor, he had faced Makkah and raised his hands. The words he had known since his first years came back to him and he'd felt the comfort of the familiar postures, the bowing, the prostration. After so many years of *madressah*, it had settled into his limbs. He'd felt again the tranquillity that had been his at the start of Ramadan.

His prayer was simple:

Guide me, Allah. Guide me.

He was still thinking about his dream and what it could mean when he got out of the school gates and saw Skrooz's car parked up. His heart sank.

Usually, the car was packed with the other lads but today Skrooz was on his own. "Just you and me today, Fraz," he said as he opened the car door for Faraz.

Faraz nodded. By now, he was used to doing as he was told.

★ ★ ★

The flat was dim, all the curtains drawn. Once Faraz's eyes had adjusted to the gloom, he saw a black bag, overflowing with rubbish, standing by the front door, waiting to be taken downstairs. Fruit flies buzzed around it and the smell of rotting garbage hung in the air.

"Wait here," Skrooz said curtly before turning to walk down the short corridor.

Faraz stood by the front door for a moment, listening out for any sounds that would give a hint about the flat's inhabitants. Beyond the faint pattering of the rain outside, he couldn't hear anything, so he stepped forward towards the door that stood in front of him.

He pushed it open and nearly fainted at the stench that greeted him. A putrid blend of stale curry, sweat, urine and that sickly sweet smell from the car invaded his nostrils, bringing tears to his eyes. The carpet, where it could be seen, was covered in brown patches and the walls sprouted black and green spots where the damp was rising. Take-away containers, old newspapers, clothes and empty packets of food and drink lay everywhere. Faraz had never seen such a mess in his life.

But there was a clear space around the dark green sofa in the centre of the room. The only thing there was a plate on which were arranged, with the utmost precision, a set of syringes, a metal spoon and a lighter.

Faraz stepped back out of the room, his mind reeling. Skrooz's brother was a junkie?

He stood still for a moment, unsure of what to do. He knew Skrooz had told him to stay put but he couldn't resist finding out more about Skrooz's brother.

Slowly, he walked towards the door he had seen Skrooz push open a few minutes before. It was still slightly ajar. Holding his breath, Faraz, leant over and peered through the crack in the door.

Skrooz's brother was spread out on the unmade bed, his eyes half closed, his hair and beard long and matted, his arm riddled with holes. Skrooz was calling his name softly, trying to rouse him. Anwar's bloodshot eyes fluttered open. He took a while to focus and recognise his brother, who kept talking to him in a calm, low voice.

"Have you brought me some smack, Khalid?" His feeble voice sounded like it was being squeezed out of his throat. "Have you brought me some, bro?"

Skrooz simply nodded as he helped him to sit up, pull on a jumper, push his feet into slippers.

When Anwar saw the bag of brown powder, his lips spread into a grin, revealing black holes where his teeth should have been.

"*Alhamdulillah...*" he breathed happily as he pulled out a plate, similar to the one in the living room, and began to prepare his fix. All of a sudden, he was animated, full of questions about family and friends.

"How's Mam, Khalid? Is her knee still bothering her? How is Ramzan going? I really miss her biryani, y'know..."

Skrooz, Khalid, answered all his brother's questions patiently as he started to pick up some of the dirty clothes that covered the floor.

"Yeah, Ramzan's going fine, Uncle Abbas is coming up from London for Eid and our mum is dead pleased…"

They carried on in this way, Skrooz totally transformed from a street thug to a good Pakistani family boy. The change was too much for Faraz, who backed away from the door, stumbling on his way back to the front door where he was supposed to have been standing.

This is too mad, thought Faraz. *Just surreal.*

What was this crazy underworld where guys with names like Khalid picked up English girls for a bit of fun then talked about marrying a good Pakistani girl, where bearded junkies in *shalwar kameez* praised God when they got a fix, where smoking, drugs, robbery and more took place during the sacred month of Ramadan, while others prayed and fasted. It was like living in the twilight zone.

And as Faraz thought of all he had seen, done and heard since the start of Ramadan, during which he had experienced the highest and lowest points of his life, the smell of the rubbish bin hit him again and his stomach lurched.

"Skrooz!" he called out suddenly. "I'm just going to take this rubbish out, yeah?"

There was a muffled sound from the room which Faraz took to be an 'OK' and, seconds later, he was out of the front door, in a corner of the stairwell, retching.

This can't go on, he thought miserably. *I can't keep this up.*

When his stomach had settled, he stepped back into the house and picked up the bin bag and stuffed it down into the shute. He waited and listened as it fell down, down, down and crashed onto the other bags of rubbish waiting at the bottom. He could hear the splintering of glass as some bottles broke on impact.

That's me, he thought to himself. *I'm falling down, further and further. It's only a matter of time before I crash too, just like that bag of rubbish.*

When Skrooz came downstairs, he found Faraz, white-faced, soaking wet, standing next to the car.

"What's the matter with you?" he growled. All traces of the Khalid Faraz had seen looking after his heroin-addicted brother had disappeared.

"Nothing, man, nothing."

Skrooz did not speak to him again while he loaded the back of the car with his cousin's dirty laundry.

They drove until they reached an intersection. The lights were red. Faraz looked idly to the side, trying to see through the trails of water on the window. The car in the next lane was a red Mini Cooper. The driver was wearing a *niqab*. Their eyes met and Faraz saw that she recognised him. Then he saw her gaze shift towards the driver's face.

He couldn't see her expression but, the next thing he knew, the lights were green and Auntie Najma had pulled away with a screech of car tyres.

Skrooz dropped him off at the end of his street. "See you tomorrow morning, yeah?" he called after him. "Got to drop something off for me before school, OK?"

Faraz said nothing. He just nodded his head and turned to walk up the road to his house. But as he walked towards his gate, he saw the red Mini parked up.

Auntie Najma leaned out.

"*Asalaamu alaikum*, Faraz," she called out. "I need to speak to you."

For the first time in his life, Faraz did not want to talk to his aunt. He looked over at his front door.

"Ummm, Auntie, d'you think it could wait? Ammiji's expecting me y'see…"

"No, Faraz, it can't wait." She looked at him hard. "Get in the car."

He opened the passenger door and got in, avoiding her eyes as he wiped the rain from his forehead.

"We're going for a drive," said his aunt as she looked in the rear view mirror and began to reverse.

They drove in silence until they had left Faraz's street far behind.

At last, Auntie Najma spoke. "Faraz," she began, "what are you doing hanging out with someone like Skrooz?"

"Skrooz?" Faraz squeaked, sweat springing up under his collar. "Oh, nothing, just hanging out, that's all. I don't really know him that well, we just…"

Auntie Najma slammed the brakes and the car lurched to a halt.

"Don't lie to me, Faraz!" Faraz had never

hear his aunt raise her voice and he stared at her. He saw that she had tears in her eyes and that her hands on the steering wheel were trembling. "Don't you dare lie to me!" she said again, her voice shaking. "Not now!"

Faraz didn't know what to say. Several times he opened his mouth to speak but no sound came out. Where to begin? How much to say? And then Faraz felt a wave of shame wash over him as he remembered that rainy afternoon, so like this one and so unlike it too, when they had first spoken about the potential of Ramadan and a fire had been lit inside him.

He felt tears prick his eyes as he looked away from his aunt. There was no way he could tell her.

Then came her voice, deep and gravelly as ever. "I know, Faraz. I know."

He whipped round to face her, his face pale, his mouth open.

"I know what Skrooz gets you to do, I know what he wants from you. I know him, Faraz, better than you ever will..."

"Know him?" Faraz choked on the words. "How?"

Auntie Najma sighed and lifted her *niqab*.

Faraz saw that the rain outside and the steamy windows meant that no one could see into the car.

"Faraz, I once knew a boy who was just like you: beautiful, sensitive, shy. He lived next door to me and our parents were friends. The other boys gave him a hard time because he wasn't like them but I didn't care. He was my friend and I loved him.

"Anyway, we moved away from that neighbourhood and I didn't hear from him for a long time. We grew up, I guess, went to different schools, got into different things and lost touch. But I never forgot him and, in my daydreams, I would dream that he came to look for me and that we got married and lived happily every after – my own fairy tale come true...."

She laughed at herself then, and wiped her nose before continuing.

"Well, Faraz, you may have heard your mum and aunts talking about when I hit my teenage years, how I turned into a total rebel. But my parents didn't know half the stuff I got up to. I used to hang out with a group of girls at school and, together, we got up to all sorts."

Faraz stared at his aunt. She glanced at him and continued.

"I know what it's like, Faraz, to want to belong, to want to be like everyone else, to want to taste that life, that crazy, carefree life that our parents tried to keep us away from. So, my parents never saw anything other than me going to school in my *shalwar kameez* and *dupatta*, and coming home with homework. They never really took an interest in my schoolwork, so it was easy to hang out down the town centre instead of going to lessons – none of us liked school anyway. This was our taste of freedom and we didn't care.

"Anyway, it was around that time that I first met Khalid – Skrooz's real name – through a friend. He was a big shot, even then, and he was the hottest guy around. Of course, I thought it was great that he fancied me…"

Faraz interrupted, fearful of what she was going to say. "Auntie, you didn't…"

"Let me finish, Faraz. I can't deny, I was seduced by the money and the cars – all the excitement – and I led him on for a while, enjoying the attention. He used to drive me around with him when I was supposed to be at school, showing off the whole time about how big he was going to be, how much money he would have someday, and all that.

"Anyway, one day, I was in a newsagent's shop, picking up some drinks while Khalid waited outside in the car. I turned to walk up one of the aisles and stopped short. There was a guy in there, about my age, but really rough-looking. His clothes looked like they hadn't been changed for days and his hair was long and matted. I stepped back when the smell hit me – but then he turned my way and I almost fainted…"

"Why, Auntie?"

Najma squeezed her eyes shut as the image that had haunted her all these years appeared before her: the face, so familiar, and yet so changed. The pale, rough skin, the bloodshot eyes, the haunted stare. Those eyes… those eyes….

"Anwar…" she breathed.

Faraz felt the blood drain from his face.

Najma told Faraz what had happened next. How she had called his name and he had turned to her, staring, recognising, trembling with shame, pulling his cardigan around his thin shoulders.

"That was all that was left of my childhood friend, the Anwar of my dreams: an empty, broken shell. 'Anwar, what happened?' I asked him. 'Who did this to you? Tell me!'"

Anwar's eyes had left Najma's face then to settle on the face that loomed behind her. He'd opened his mouth to speak, but Skrooz's voice had cut him off.

'Go home, Anwar,' he had growled. 'You look a mess...'

"'*You*?' I screamed. '*You* did this to him?'

"Khalid – Skrooz – sneered then, so full of himself. 'It's not my fault that he was dumb enough to start tasting the stuff himself... that's what happens to pretty boys who ain't got no brains...'

"How I hated him at that moment. All I could think of was my friend, Anwar, who used to make up stories with me, build castles in the sand, taught me how to ride a bike and promised not to tell when I broke the neighbour's fence. And I thought of his mum, his Ammiji – he had always been her favourite – and his father who had been so proud of him when he won the athletics at primary school.

"I could feel my heart breaking – the waste! And I saw then where Skrooz got his power from: sucking the life out of everyone around him.

"I began to shout at him then, crying, screaming, beating him with my fists. He held my wrists and tried to get me to control myself, to scare me.

But I was wild with rage. Everyone in the shop was staring but I didn't care. Finally, Khalid managed to bundle me out of the shop and into his car but I was still screaming at him. I saw Anwar come out of the shop and I made to open the door, calling his name. I wanted to run back to him, to help him, to take him back home to his mum and dad.

"But Khalid grabbed me by my arm and shook me. 'He's finished, Najma!' he bellowed. 'That's life! Now shut up and get a grip before I really give it to ya!' He got a fistful of my hair and held it tight as he started the car. He only let go when I stopped screaming Anwar's name.

"That was the last time I ever saw Anwar. I don't know where he is now. But that day was a turning point for me. It was like I had been to the Dark Side – and I didn't want the dark any more. I wanted out. So that was when I stopped hanging out and starting looking into 6th form and universities. I wanted to get away from there, far away – I wanted something different... and I got it."

Auntie Najma took a deep breath and looked at Faraz's stunned face.

"I won't let you end up like Anwar, Faraz,

no way. Fear no one but Allah, Faraz. You have to be strong. You only get one try in this life and you are throwing it away. You have to end it with Skrooz and you have to do it today."

★ ★ ★

When Faraz got home, Mum and Dad had gone to the mosque to take food for the community iftar. He went straight to Farhana's room. He hesitated just a moment before knocking on the door.

When Farhana opened the door and saw Faraz standing there she said, "What do *you* want?"

"*Asalaamu alaikum*, sis, can I come in? I need to speak to you…"

Farhana nodded silently and let him in.

As soon as the door was closed, Faraz turned to his sister. "Farhana," he cried, "I'm so sorry, sorry for everything!" Tears sprang to his eyes at the thought of all that had happened in the past weeks.

Farhana, her heart bursting, felt tears rolling down her cheeks and she said, "Me too, Faraz, I'm sorry… so sorry…"

The twins hugged each other fiercely. It had

been hard being strangers.

"Just look at the two of us," laughed Farhana through her tears. "Imagine if the lads could see you now!"

At that, Faraz drew back and became serious. "Nah, sis, I'm finished with Skrooz and his crew. It's over."

And he told Farhana everything, everything that had been happening in the last few weeks, everything Auntie Najma had told him.

As he spoke, Farhana grew paler and paler. And then they both heard the familiar screech of tyres come to a stop outside their gate.

They looked at each other, neither of them saying a word.

Then Faraz took a deep breath. "It's now or never," he murmured.

Farhana nodded, her eyes wide. She got up and followed him down the stairs to the front door.

The streetlights reflected off the rain and Farhana couldn't make out the faces of the people sitting in the car. She saw Faraz with his hood up, talking to the driver. She saw him shake his head several times, shrug his shoulders then open his arms out wide, a gesture of defiance. Then the car engine revved a few times and the big black BMW sped off down the street.

Farhana tried to read the expression on Faraz's wet face when he got back into the house but he avoided her gaze.

"Faraz?" she said softly.

Faraz put his arm around his sister. "It'll be all right now, *insha Allah*," he said thickly. "It's over."

But his heart was still pounding and he could still hear Skrooz's voice as he hissed: *"You're gonna regret this, mate. Just you wait and see…"*

On the way to school the next morning, he tossed his new mobile phone, the gift from Skrooz, into a roadside bin. And he kept walking.

Chapter 18

Collision

Farhana was running late. That morning Faraz had been the one struggling to wake her up. She had eaten like a zombie and had gone back to sleep afterwards. She had woken up with a splitting headache, even groggier than she had been before. Her limbs felt like lead as she washed and dressed, knowing that she was already late for school.

She brushed her hair and tied it up in a hair elastic.

She smiled when she thought about her brother and how good it had felt to be talking again, but her smile faded as her eyes flickered up towards the white scarf. She hesitated. Would she wear it today? Could she be bothered? What if she didn't wear it? She'd be a laughing stock, that's for sure. It was bad enough to ruin your image by starting to cover up, it was worse to stop wearing it because you couldn't handle the pressure.

She was glad Faraz had dealt with Skrooz, but she realised with a sigh that it didn't make much difference to her and her issues.

She took a deep breath and pulled the scarf off the side of the mirror. She avoided looking at herself as she pinned it under her chin. *That girl in the mirror isn't me,* she thought sourly. *I don't look like that inside….*

She picked up her bag and left the room without looking back.

★ ★ ★

The day dragged for Farhana. Shazia tried to get her to talk but gave up when she realised that Farhana was determined to be depressed. Even Robina avoided antagonising her, preferring to play to her adoring fans instead.

They were all talking about Eid, which was now in one week's time: what they were going to wear, where they were going to go, what presents they were hoping for.

Farhana ignored them all, losing herself in

her dark and dreary thoughts.

I feel like Ramadan is already over for me...

★ ★ ★

At Middleton Comprehensive, Faraz was on top of the world. All day long, since dropping his phone in the bin, he had been buoyed by a sense of freedom, of exhilaration, of endless possibilities.

He had scored decent marks in his maths test, he had totally understood what the Science teacher was talking about for once and he had managed to make his noon prayer on time.

As he finished praying, he noticed that one of the other boys was still in the room. He turned to him and saw that he was one of the boys he had seen going to the *tarawih* prayers, at the beginning of Ramadan.

"*Asalaamu alaikum,*" he said, surprised at his own boldness.

"*Wa alaikum salaam,* bro," the boy smiled. His moustache was just starting to come through and he had bright, intelligent eyes. "Haven't seen you much around here lately... you been busy?"

"Yeah," Faraz blushed, thinking about Skrooz.

"I have been a bit busy. But all that's over now – I think I'll be here a lot more."

"You're the one who did that Arabic calligraphy that's up in the art room, right?"

"Yeah, that's right," Faraz replied. "How do you know about that?"

"Mr McCarthy was raving about it – he wouldn't stop going on about you!"

Faraz smiled. "That's nothing! Have you heard of Ahmed Ali, the Muslim graffiti artist?"

"Is he the one who did that mural down the town centre? Yeah, my sister is a huge fan – I think one of her friends told her about it so she dragged me down there. It was pretty cool... could you do that, d'you think?"

Faraz thought for a moment then said, "I could give it a try... I would love to do something that massive..."

The two boys fell silent, lost in their private thoughts, comfortable in the unexpected camaraderie. Then they both heard the bell go and the boy said, "Listen, bro, I have to go... see you around *insha Allah*."

"Yeah, man, see you around..." They shook hands and the boy picked up his bag and walked to the door.

"Hey, man, what's your name?"

"Sameer," said the boy with a smile. "And you're Faraz, right?"

Faraz grinned and nodded.

"See you around, bro, stay cool…"

And he was gone.

Mr McCarthy gave Faraz permission to stay after school to work on his coursework. Once again, Faraz was in the zone. His brain buzzed with a thousand and one images as he applied paint to canvas, slapping, smearing and teasing the surface until he achieved the effect he was looking for. Mr McCarthy sat at the back of the class, catching up on paperwork, listening to opera on his portable cassette player. Now and again, he came over to where Faraz was working to observe his progress. He would turn away, smiling. He was glad Faraz was back. He hoped it was for good this time.

For Faraz, the outside world ceased to exist as he worked away, stopping only to pray the mid-afternoon prayer. When at last he stood back to get a better view of his painting, he was pleased with what he saw. It was shaping up beautifully.

A couple more sessions like this and he would be ready to hand it in.

"Ok, Sir, I think I'm done for today," he called over to his teacher.

Mr McCarthy looked up, blinking through his thick glasses. "It's looking great, Faraz, really amazing... so much energy and feeling. I can't wait to see the finished product."

"Neither can I," replied Faraz as he packed away his pencils. "See you tomorrow, Sir."

"Yes, Faraz," replied his teacher, "see you tomorrow."

Faraz left Mr McCarthy still gazing at his picture, his long, delicate fingers resting on his chin.

How did he ever end up in a dump like this? he thought to himself.

By the time Faraz left the school gates, the sun was dipping. He hummed to himself as he crossed the car park towards the bus stop, reciting phrases of *Qur'an* as he bounced across the tarmac.

Alhamdulillah, he couldn't remember having a better day, a day where everything had been so easy! Judging by the late afternoon sunlight, it would soon be time to break his fast. He would try to get home in time to break with his mum and Farhana.

Farhana! He jammed his hand into his pocket to get his phone. He was suddenly overwhelmed by the urge to speak to her, to ask her how her day went, where she was. But his pocket was empty. He groaned when he remembered that he had thrown away his phone that morning. He would have to wait until he got home.

He was so engrossed in his thoughts about Farhana and his great day that he didn't notice Maj and the three lads he had with him, standing at the end of the street, waiting, waiting.

* * *

Farhana decided to go to the library on her way home. Not her local library but the big library in town, the one with the coffee shop downstairs and the mall next door.

"You sure you don't want me to come with you?" Shazia was reluctant to let her go on her own.

"No thanks, Shaz, I'll be fine," Farhana replied. "Besides, it's better you don't. You know your dad doesn't like you going down the town centre…"

"Yeah, I know, but still…"

"No, it's not worth it, Shazia, I'm just going to pop into the library and read for a bit, maybe window shop and stuff. I just need to clear my head."

"Ok, then, Farhana, you just call me if you need anything, OK?"

The two girls hugged each other, then turned towards opposite ends of the street to take their buses.

Farhana looked out of the window as the bus trundled along. She saw a poster for the latest copy of Asian Girl magazine on the side of a bus stop: two tall, slim, long-haired beauties, dressed in the latest Asian fashion. With their blue contacts, pale make-up and teased hairstyles, they looked just like white girls, hardly Asian at all. Outside the bus window, on billboards, bus stops, magazine covers and shop windows, a hundred images of beautiful women, glamorous women, impossibly perfect women, flew past. It was as it they were mocking her: 'Don't you wish you looked like this?'

And yet, just a few short weeks ago, she had been compared to those models, those singers, those movie stars. And now? She was out of the running, her *hijab* a big white banner announcing to the world that she had opted out of the competition.

A part of her missed that competition, a competition she had won when Malik fell for her.

But what was it worth at the end of the day? Hadn't she seen through the shallowness of all that and made a conscious decision to wear *hijab*, to be a better Muslim?

Hadn't she come to her senses about Malik?

Her thoughts consumed her as she got off the bus and walked towards the library. She was so lost in thought that she was halfway to the library when she looked up and saw a tall Asian lad with a floppy mop of hair and a caramel complexion, and a girl in school uniform with highlights in her hair. And her heart stopped beating.

It was Malik and Robina.

★ ★ ★

"Oi! Fraz!" Maj's voice rang out from the end of the suddenly deserted street. He and the other lads had started walking towards Faraz, slowly, their hands behind their backs. Walking beside each other, they filled the street and cut him off from the bus stop.

Faraz's heart began to thump and the blood rushed to his head, roaring in his ears. These lads were big, very big. A quick glance confirmed his worst fears: they were all armed. He could see the shapes of bats, and he caught the glimmer of a knife.

"We've got some unfinished business, you and me." Maj's voice was thick with menace. "Skrooz isn't here to save you, Pretty Boy. And now you're going to see what happens when you mess with the big boys."

Faraz took one look at him, caught the rage shining in his eyes, the ugly scar on his face, turned and ran for his life.

"After him, lads!" roared Maj and, like one body, they sprang after Faraz.

The chase was on.

★ ★ ★

Farhana stopped in her tracks and let out a tiny, stifled cry. So Robina had been telling the truth after all. When her heart began to beat again, it pounded in her chest, painfully, her mouth dry.

She stepped behind a pillar, out of sight. All those times of missing Malik, of wanting to hear his voice, of wishing they were back together came flooding back, bringing tears to her eyes.

You're an idiot, Farhana, just like Robina said.

But her curiosity got the better of her and she willed herself to look out from behind the pillar. From there, she could see that something was up. Malik's body language was all wrong. For a start, he wasn't smiling. One of his hands gripped his school bag and the other stabbed the air around Robina's shoulder.

Farhana just could not resist. Silently, keeping her head down, she wove her way through the crowd of shoppers until she was behind the pillar closest to them. From there, she could hear Malik's voice clearly. But it certainly was not the voice she was used to, the one that made her think of melted chocolate. This voice was hard, cold. This was a Malik she didn't know.

"So what did you call me here for, Robina?"

he was saying. "Why did you say you were with Farhana?" Then he looked at her suspiciously. He knew why she had played that trick on him. "How many times do I have to tell you?" he growled. "I'm just not interested, OK? I wish you'd drop it cos you're starting to get on my nerves! It's bad enough you ringing up all my mates, but tricking me into meeting you? That's just pathetic! I'm not into you, get it?"

Farhana saw Robina's cheeks flare up and recognised the stubborn set of her chin.

"Malik, who are you trying to fool? I've seen the way you look at me. Besides," she arched her eyebrow, "do you know how many guys would kill for a piece of me?"

"Yeah, well not this guy." And he turned to leave.

But Robina wasn't finished. She called out after him, her voice taunting, "Is that because you're still pining for Farhana? Cos she broke your heart?"

Malik stopped and turned back towards Robina who shook her head, smiling. "Poor Malik... you picked the wrong girl to fall for, eh? The ice maiden herself... you should have seen her face when I told her about you and Amber at that party...."

Malik's face twisted. "Me and *who*?"

"Well, it seemed like a good enough story: you and a model hooking up at a party, a party she wasn't allowed to go to…"

"Are you talking about Imti's party, the one where you tried to…"

"Well, I couldn't tell her that, could I?"

The enormity of Robina's words began to dawn on Malik and his face clouded with anger. He grabbed Robina by the arm and said, through gritted teeth, "What d'you tell her that for? Huh? So that she'd finish with me?"

But Robina glared at him, her eyes flashing. "Oh, get real, Malik! She could never give you what you want! You don't need Farhana…."

"Well I definitely don't need a lying tramp like you!" He spat the words out and let go of her arm, pushing her aside as he charged past.

He was so angry that, when he looked up to see where he was going, he did not recognise the girl in the *hijab* staring at him. But there was no mistaking the green eyes and skin the colour of a latte, with a hint of mocha, even when surrounded by the unfamiliar white scarf that now hid her hair and neck from view.

As he said the name, he could hardly believe it was her.

"Farhana?"

★ ★ ★

The soles of Faraz's trainers slapped the pavement as he ran and, behind him, six other pairs of trainers slammed the ground as the lads thundered after him, hurling abuse.

Dark clouds were gathering in the late afternoon sky. If he could get into the alleyways and the industrial park near the railway line before the street lights came on, he might just make it. So he kept running, dodging past an old lady with her wheelie bag and a couple of school kids. They stared after him and the other guys, open-mouthed, their hands full of sweets.

Then, out of the corner of his eye, he saw a familiar figure on the other side of the road. It was Shazia! He couldn't manage more than a glance in her direction as he sped past and he saw her call out to him – then freeze at the sight of the boys pursuing him. Within moments, he had left her far behind.

It had been a long time since he had run this fast. And he hadn't eaten since before dawn. He could feel the strength begin to drain out of his body. He looked behind him and saw that Maj and another tall lad were gaining on him. He would have to shake them. Seeing an alleyway to his left, he quickly turned and ran along it, scraping his arm on the wall as he squeezed past an abandoned car with flat tyres. He could hear Maj and the other boy calling after him, their voices bouncing off the alley walls.

But the alley was a dead end. Ahead of him was a wall, a high wall, too high to jump over. There was no escape.

He turned to face them and was immediately knocked backwards off his feet by the power of Maj's angry fists. Pain shot through his body, like fireworks, exploding, ending in a shower of stars. He didn't know what was hitting him or where. At first he tried to hit out, to fight back but he eventually retreated to covering his face with his arms, his hands holding his head, curled up in the foetal position as the fists, bats and boots beat a rhythm on his body.

All of a sudden, through the din, he heard Maj

shout, "Enough!" And the beating stopped.

Faraz stayed curled up on the floor, the scent of blood, sweat and tarmac filling his nostrils.

Maj pushed him over with his foot and stood on his shoulder pinning him down. Faraz cried out with pain and tried to break free but Maj knelt down until his face was inches from his. Maj smiled and his scar twisted as the skin pulled.

"Now, Pretty Boy" he hissed softly, "let me show you what an artist I can be..." He took something out of his back pocket.

And Faraz saw the lamplight glint off the switchblade's sharp edge.

He closed his eyes then.

O Allah, help me now!

He felt the knife point press into the skin under his eye and the searing pain as the blade sliced his skin.

★ ★ ★

The mall and everything in it began to sway and move in slow motion when Farhana looked into Malik's eyes. He was only a few steps away so she could see his face clearly, could read the expression in his eyes. The shock of recognition, then the blur of incomprehension was clearly etched on his face.

He took slow steps towards her, his eyes searching hers for an explanation, for a sign. "Farhana?" he whispered, his voice hoarse, so unlike his usual self-assured tone.

"Yes, Malik," she answered softly, "it's me."

Malik's eyes swept over the white scarf, the bare nails, the long skirt.

"What...?" He couldn't find the right words to say. "Where did you go? Why didn't you return any of my calls? What's happened to you?"

He looked behind him and saw Robina standing there, an arch look on her face.

"See what you've been pining for, Malik?" she purred. "There's nothing there any more..."

"Robina, get lost!" he shouted at her.

Farhana saw her triumphant façade crumble and she seemed to shrink slightly. Still, she put on a brave face as she looked over at Farhana.

"I guess he really *is* crazy about you, huh? So, you've won..."

"Robina, would you just shut up!" Farhana glared at her one-time friend. "There are no winners here, don't you understand? We're playing a losers' game, all of us. The saddest thing about you is that you refuse to see that. To be honest, I pity you. You're trying so hard to become your sister that you're losing yourself – and everything that we ever liked about you. I suggest you take a long hard look at what is really important in your life and fix up before it's too late."

"I-I don't need to take this from you!" spluttered Robina. "Who do you think you are anyway?"

"I was, *am*, your friend, Robina, and I'm the only one with the guts to tell you what everyone else can see. You'd better take it from me before it's too late and you find yourself stuck in your own delusions, surrounded by haters and fakers who don't give a damn about you!"

Farhana saw the hurt in Robina's eyes before she hardened them and tossed her hair out of her face and put her hand up to Farhana.

"Whatever!" she snapped before stalking off towards the entrance.

Farhana watched her go. Robina had a huge ego and was prouder than a peacock, but she wasn't dumb. Hopefully, she would come round...

"Farhana..?" Her attention turned back to Malik. As she turned to him, a lock of hair slipped out from beneath her white cotton headscarf. Malik reached over and she closed her eyes as she felt her hair, and his fingers brush her face as he pushed it back.

She could have him back now if she wanted, she knew that. All she had to say was 'yes'. Her heart formed the words before her mouth opened.

"No, Malik," she said at last. "I can't."

Malik's face fell. "Is it because of Robina?" he asked then. "That stuff she told you, it wasn't even true! It's you I want. You're all I ever wanted...."

Farhana's heart clenched.

Oh, what a test. What a test!

But she took a deep breath, swallowed hard. "I'm sorry, Malik," she said. "When Robina told me about you and that girl, I didn't know what to think. I'd always known that I was taking huge risks by getting involved with you – or anyone! But her story seemed to confirm that I was doing the wrong thing. That it wasn't worth it; that *you* weren't worth it....

"But this scarf, my Islam, doesn't have anything to do with all that, not really. This is about me. This Ramadan has made me think about a lot of things and I've decided I want to be a proper

Muslim, not just in name, but in what I do as well. I know that must be hard for you to understand but maybe you will someday..."

But Malik wasn't having it. Farhana flinched when she saw the angry hurt in his eyes. "You know what? It *is* hard for me to understand! I *love* you! How can that be wrong?"

Farhana turned away then, trying to hide her face.

"Farhana, look at me! You're trying to make this into something ugly, like I'm sort of perv or something. You know those things I said to you, those things I wrote? I have *never* said them to any other girl, ever! People look at me and think, 'yeah, he must have girls throwing themselves at him, he must get around,' but they don't know me. They don't know that I'm not into all that. You know me – you should have known better than to believe a girl like Robina..."

"Malik, what do you want me to say?" Farhana was shouting now. "You know the rules; you know that, as far as our religion is concerned, we shouldn't even be seeing each other! So what, you want to *marry* me now? Get me to run away with you? Can't you see? It's a dead end, Malik, a dead end..."

"No, Farhana," he replied, "it doesn't have to be a dead end! We can make this work, I swear we can..."

"How can it work, Malik?" Farhana asked sadly. "Look at me. I've come so far. I'm praying, I'm wearing *hijab*, I'm trying to do what I should as a Muslim. And I'm happy like this. We're not on the same wavelength any more, Malik. We want different things, you know we do..."

Malik listened, not saying a word. When he spoke, his voice was thick with emotion. "I want to change your mind. I love you and part of me doesn't give a damn about whether it's right or not."

Then his voice fell and he looked away.

"But then I know that you're right. That you're doing the right thing. I know our religion as well as you do. And I know you: once you've decided something, that's it."

When he looked up at her again, his eyes shone with tears and a new respect.

"You always were the strong one, Farhana, no doubt. That's what makes you so special..." And he turned away, his eyes shut, fists clenched. "I'd better go..."

"No!" Farhana's heart cried out in agony. But she bit her lip and kept silent, even as every muscle in her body strained to call him back.

Bismillah. This is the way it must be.

"Malik!" she called out when he was a few steps away. "*Asalaamu alaikum*?"

"*Wa alaikum salaam*," he replied over his shoulder and, after one last look, he walked away into the crowd.

As Farhana walked out of the mall, into the street, the wind whipped the tears from her eyes.

Or it could have been the raindrops as they fell, splattering, from the heavy skies.

★ ★ ★

Faraz was lulled by the motion of the car. He couldn't quite believe that he was on his way home in a car with Shazia, the girl of his dreams, and with Imran, not after what had happened. His mind ran over the events of the past thirty minutes.

Just as Maj had started to carve up his face, they had heard a voice, loud and gruff, bouncing off the alley walls.

"Oi, what's going on over there?!"

Three policemen and a community officer were at the bottom of the alleyway. With them, panting and out of breath was a pretty, plump girl in a black scarf – Shazia.

Maj's boys had all scattered like cockroaches as the policemen began to run towards them. They had used the bins to clamber over the wall and make their escape. A couple of the officers had climbed the wall after them.

In a moment, Faraz was surrounded by uniforms and strong, reassuring arms. He had tried hard to focus and then the community officer's face swam into view. It was Imran, the director of the Muslim youth art organisation.

"Faraz?" Imran was incredulous. "What happened, bro? Who did this?"

But Faraz just shook his head. He didn't want to talk.

"Where's Shazia?" he asked, shakily.

"This young lady was very brave," said one of the officers. "She's the one who found us and told us what was going on. It's safe to say that, if she hadn't, you would be in a right state by now…"

"Shazia?" Faraz whispered, gazing up at her.

"You saved my life?"

"No, silly," she said, softly, "just your face…"

Faraz's heart sang with joy in spite of his aching limbs. Now all he wanted was to get home. But the policemen wanted some details before dropping him home.

Then Faraz became evasive. "I don't know," he kept saying. "I don't know who they were…"

At last, they let him go and asked Imran, who worked with them as a part-time Police Community Support Officer, to take Faraz and Shazia home.

"They both live near me," Imran told them.

Faraz and Shazia didn't speak in the car. Both of them felt shy now that the excitement had died away. Imran kept shaking his head, muttering to himself, talking about 'the youth'.

Faraz wasn't really listening. They dropped Shazia at her house first. Imran ran up to the door to explain why he was bringing Shazia home. At the door, Shazia gave a little wave.

"*Asalaamu alaikum*, Faraz," she called softly. "I'm glad you're OK, really glad."

Faraz grinned then winced, his head still hurting.

When they got to his road, he asked Imran to drop him a few doors down from his house.

"I need to come in and see your parents, Faraz," he said sternly.

"Oh, they won't be home now," replied Faraz uneasily.

Imran gave him a hard look. "Of all the kids I know, Faraz," he said at last, "you were the last one I expected to be mixed up in all this stuff. I won't lie: I'm well disappointed, bro. What are you covering for those idiots for? Huh? Because of some warped code of honour?"

And Faraz remembered Skrooz's expression: *izzat of the streets.*

But Imran wasn't finished: "There are too many kids throwing their lives away for this stuff, Faraz. You've got more to give than that!" He looked away and unlocked the car door. "I'll be round tomorrow to have a word with your mum and dad. You'd better go get yourself cleaned up; the police will want to talk to you again tomorrow. I hope you'll have something sensible to say to them."

And he was gone.

Faraz waited for him to go before turning towards his house.

While Faraz was walking up the street, Farhana was getting off her bus on the other side of the road. The rain fell in a steady drizzle, mingling with her tears, blurring her vision.

OK, now, pull yourself together, Farhana, she thought. *What's done is done... no regrets. Bismillah...*

There was a delivery van parked next to the bus stop and Farhana found herself behind it. Taking a deep breath, she looked across the road, getting ready to cross. And her eyes fell on a familiar figure walking towards her house. His face was lit up for a moment by the street light.

"Faraz!" she cried out, her heart soaring at the sight of him.

All she wanted to do was cry on his shoulder, to hear her tell her that she had done the right thing, that everything would be all right. She rushed out into the road to meet him.

She didn't see the car.

★ ★ ★

Just as Farhana stepped out into the street from behind the delivery van, a car's lights lit up the rain-drenched road and it screeched into motion. It took Faraz just a split second to recognise the face behind the front wheel. It was Skrooz and he was glaring right at him.

Then everything started to slow down, down, down, so that Faraz could see every little thing that happened next.

Farhana's bag as it bumped her leg as she ran out into the street.

The look of pure evil on Skrooz's face as he pointed towards him, his mouth open in a bellow that seemed to rip through Faraz's body.

How Farhana's head in its white scarf lurched backwards as the car rammed straight into her.

How her body flew through the air with dreadful grace.

How suddenly she landed on the rain-soaked ground.

The shouts and curses that rocked the air.

The car's tyres squealing, its engine revving as it reversed back down the street, away, away, into the distance.

The rain that fell on his head, drenching him as he bent over his twin sister's twisted body.

The raw fire that seared his throat as he roared up to the heavens. *"Nooooooo!"*

A roar that was swallowed up by the cries and shouts of the neighbours, the wails of his mother, the scream of sirens, the chaos.

No, Allah, no. There's no way this can be happening... no way.

To Him do we belong and to Him we shall return.

Chapter 19

Repair

Farhana was alive, but only just.

Faraz wouldn't leave her side. Ignoring repeated questions about his own bruised and swollen face and the wound under his eye, he insisted on riding with Farhana in the ambulance. He stayed with her when she was admitted to hospital, while she was given blood, while doctors ran tests, while her heart monitor bleeped and bleeped.

His parents tried to get him to take a break, to have something to eat, to calm down but he wouldn't hear of it. The guilt sat churning in his stomach as he looked at the bloodied cuts on her face, the ugly bruises on her arms, the neck brace and the cast that covered one of her legs.

This is all my fault. If I hadn't fallen in with Skrooz, if I hadn't gone after Maj, if I'd said something earlier, if I'd just been stronger, none of this would have happened …

At last, he agreed to let the staff dress his wounds and the hospital agreed to allow him and his mother to stay with Farhana overnight.

Ammiji cried quietly, holding her daughter's hand, her handkerchief balled tightly in her fist. She kept looking from her son to her daughter and back again, almost unable to recognise them.

"What happened, Faraz? Who did this to you, to your sister?" she asked through her tears.

Faraz looked at his mum and was reminded of how different her world was from theirs. She had no clue about the trials he and Farhana had faced, this Ramadan and before that. Whose fault was it? He couldn't tell. All he knew was that it wasn't right. Some things were going to have to change, even if some painful truths needed to be told. But not now. Now she needed him to be strong for her, to be the brave son she had always wanted.

"Shh, Ammiji," Faraz soothed, rubbing her back. "We'll talk about it in the morning, OK?"

At last, she fell asleep at the side of the bed. Faraz found a blanket and tenderly laid it over her, smoothing her hair off her forehead.

That night, Faraz felt as if his own heart had caught Farhana's rhythm. If there was any interruption to its beat, his heart leapt in time. He spent every moment of the night talking to her, praying, crying, whispering 'I'm sorry' over and over again.

Auntie Najma came as soon as visiting hours opened the next day. She held her elder sister-in-law for a long time, tears slipping down both their cheeks. All the tension of the previous weeks had disappeared – they were family again. Then Auntie Najma turned to Faraz and ran her hand down his face, her eyes full of questions.

Faraz shook his head and aunt and nephew embraced.

"I'll stay for as long as you need me, Uzma," she said to Faraz's mum.

Ammiji nodded.

* * *

The next morning, they all sat down with the doctor in one of the private meeting rooms.

"She's stable," said the doctor in charge of Farhana's care. "Her arm is broken and there are

249

multiple fractures in the leg. She was fortunate – her bag appears to have broken her fall or we would be talking about head injuries, possible brain damage."

Faraz and his dad held his mum as she let out a gasp and swayed slightly in her chair. "*Brain* damage?"

"So far, she is responding well and we are pleased with her progress. Please rest assured that we are doing all that we can for her."

"Thank you, doctor," said Faraz's dad, shaking his hand.

The doctor then looked at Faraz pointedly and coughed.

"We have also spoken with the police. There is concern among the staff that this accident was not random. That it was premeditated in some way – perhaps your son would know something about that?"

Ammiji's head snapped round to look at Faraz, who looked down. She turned to the doctor.

"My son?" she said, incredulously. "I'm sure you don't mean my Faraz. He has no idea how this all happened I can assure you."

The doctor raised an eyebrow. "Well, the police will be back this afternoon and they have said that they will be wanting to speak to him. Maybe you should speak to him before they do..." And with that, he left the room.

Faraz's mother was furious. She turned to her husband. "Did you hear that, Mahmood? How dare they try to imply that Faraz might know something about what happened to Farhana!"

"I've no idea, *beta*, it must be some mix-up, and you know how the police can be with young Asian boys..."

"Mahmood, Uzma," said Auntie Najma, standing up, "I'm going to check on Farhana, see that she's OK. You take all the time you need..." She looked at Faraz then. She tried to keep her expression neutral.

Faraz took a deep breath. This was it.

"Ammiji, Dad, I've got something to tell you..."

And then, haltingly at first, Faraz spoke to his parents, with more honesty than ever in his life, about Skrooz, the lads, Maj, the fights, the car crash.

They were in that room for a long time. There

were questions, shouts, accusations, and, finally, tears.

"I thought I knew our children, Mahmood," said Ammiji, sniffling. "But I was wrong... I was wrong."

"We were both wrong," said Dad, putting one hand around her and another on Faraz's shoulder.

Faraz looked at his dad, the man he had tried all his life to please and saw, for the first time, acceptance in his eyes instead of criticism. And he saw love.

"Oh, Dad," he whispered and, in a moment, they were all holding each other, tears running down their faces.

On the way back to the ward, they were stopped by a couple of police officers who asked to speak to Faraz. Remembering Imran's comments the night before, Faraz spoke to the police and told them all he knew about the accident.

The police took all the details and thanked him. "We often have trouble obtaining information about these people," said the officer in charge. "You've done a courageous thing, young man. What these lads did was despicable and we are going to make sure that they don't get away with it."

When they got back to the ward, Faraz told Auntie Najma what had happened. She slipped her arm around Faraz's and gave it a gentle squeeze. "I knew you'd come through, *masha Allah*," she said softly. "I knew you'd do the right thing."

★ ★ ★

Sitting next to Farhana on the ward, Faraz thought back to that first Ramadan morning when they had stayed up, just the two of them, reading and reciting the *Qur'an*, building each other up, sharing a feeling beyond words.

He thought about how those feelings had grown and strengthened, only to be swept aside by a moment of weakness. By wanting to fit in, rather than staying true to himself. By putting other people's opinions and expectations before God's, before Allah.

But that's what it's all about, isn't it? It's about striving and never giving up, even when you're knocked back. Cos there will always be tests, temptations, things that threaten to blow you off course, sacrifices to be

made. You just have to stay strong and keep fighting.
That's what it's all about.

★ ★ ★

Faraz didn't go to school for the whole week. So he was there when Farhana opened her eyes for the first time, just after the dawn prayer on the last day of Ramadan.

Faraz jumped up from his prayer mat and rushed to her side and took her hand, looking into her eyes, searching for a spark of recognition.

Farhana hesitated as she looked into his face and, for one awful moment, he thought that she didn't know who he was. Then her face eased into a smile and she squeezed his hand gently.

"*Asalaamu alaikum,* little brother," she whispered softly, her voice rough and parched but tender all the same. "You look a bit rough."

Faraz could hardly speak, he was so happy.

"You don't look so hot yourself, you know," he smiled. Then his face changed, softened. "You're going to be just fine, sis, just fine," he murmured. "I spoke to Mum and Dad. I told them everything. Things are going to be different from now on."

Farhana smiled and nodded, a tear trickling from her eye. "*Insha Allah…*" she whispered.

"I'm going to go and get them, OK?" Faraz turned to go, then stopped. "Oh, Shazia came to see you yesterday and she brought you this letter. Didn't say who it was from but said to give it to you as soon as you came to." He handed her a small white envelope then went out of the door.

Farhana struggled a little opening the envelope. But when she saw the handwriting, she stopped. Carefully, she pulled out the card. There was just a short message. Just a few lines.

Farhana, did you think I would let you go, just like that? You must think me a bigger fool than I am. Wait for me. I'm going to get myself sorted, then I'll be back for you. Someone like you only comes by once in a lifetime. I'm not about to lose you.
Insha Allah,
M.

So, when the rest of the family came in to see her, they found Farhana beaming, her eyes bright, almost as bright as the sun that rose outside the hospital window, shining on the urban Islamic mural that blazed across the wall on the other side of the road.

Shukr, it said: gratitude.

And on that last day of Ramadan, the day before Eid, Faraz, Farhana and their mother and father realised just how much they had to be grateful for as they embarked on the next stage of their journey, together.

Glossary of Words and Phrases

Some of the words in this glossary have Arabic roots, and others are in Urdu, the family language of Faraz and Farhana

Abayah outer garment

Alhamdulillah Praise be to God

Allahu akbar God is great

Ammiji Mum (Urdu)

Asalaamu alaikum peace be upon you
    (Muslim greeting)

Asr mid afternoon prayer

Azan call to prayer

Beta term of endearment (Urdu)

Bismillah in the name of God

Burqa garment that covers the whole body

Chaat Asian condiment

Deen Religion, way of life

Desi of Southeast Asian origin

Dhuhr midday prayer

Dupatta scarf worn as part of shalwar kameez
    outfit

Fajr dawn prayer

Gora/gori white person (male/female)

Haram forbidden

Hijab Islamic covering, often refers to headscarf

Hijabi someone who wears a scarf

Iftar meal eaten at sunset to break the fast

Imam leader of mosque congregation

Iman faith

Insha Allah God willing

Isha night prayer

Izzat honour (Urdu)

Jilbab loose, flowing garment worn over normal
   clothes

Karela Asian vegetable

Kurta Asian tunic top

Madressah Qur'anic school

Maghrib sunset prayer

Masha Allah it is as God intended (used when
   complimenting)

Mooli Asian vegetable

Namaz prayer (Urdu)

Niqab face veil

Pakhora Asian snack

Paneer Asian cheese

Purdah seclusion or full covering (Urdu)

Qu'ran holy book of Islam

Rakat a unit of the Muslim prayer

Ramadan sacred month of fasting

Ramadan Mubarak a Ramadan greeting

Roti Asian flat bread

Sapodilla Asian fruit

Sehri meal eaten before dawn, before the fast
    commences

Shalwar kameez traditional Asian outfit consisting
    of tunic and wide trousers

SubhanAllah glory be to God

Surahs chapters in the Qur'an

Tarawih night prayer said in Ramadan

Tasleem greeting said at the end of the prayers

Wa alaikum salaam (reply to greeting) Upon you
    be peace

Wali guardian

Wudu ablution made before prayer

Turn the page for an extract
from Na'ima B. Robert's brilliant
new novel, to be published in 2012 –

Far From Home

A prince is a slave when far from his kingdom.
Shona proverb

Tarito
Rhodesia 1975

I miss my mother. Amai.

I miss her smile and her soft voice. I miss the way she used to call me 'mwanangu', my child. I miss home.

This is not home. Home is where the earth beneath your feet is yours to till, to sow seeds, to reap the harvest, the fruit of your bare hands. The home left to you by your ancestors. We left that home long ago.

But even now, when I close my eyes, I can still see everything clearly, etched forever in my heart. The mud plaster hut with the thatched roof where I used to sleep; the great tree in the middle of the compound where Sekuru used to tell us stories of children taken away by witches, riding on the backs of hyenas; the fields of maize and the herds of sharp-horned cattle; the granite-topped mountains; the upside-down baobab tree; the endless sky, heavy with hopeful clouds at the start of the rainy season.

There is no time to look for rain clouds here. There is no point. Now we live to die, not to sow seeds and help cows give birth to calves that will one day pay roora for daughters yet to come. Now my home is the bush and my family is my comrades. My bed changes every night as we follow the signs left for us by the savannah.

Some days nothing happens, other days the earth shakes to the rhythm of land mines, limbs are lost, blood is spilled and my heart cannot stop flooding with terror. But I am strong, like my mother, and I cry my tears on the inside.

Will I ever see my home again? I do not know.

Will I ever see my father again? I do not know.

Will life ever be the same again? I do not know.

But it comforts me, comforts me and pains me, to think of how it came to this, how I came to call the bush my home.

So I will think of it now. I will remember everything that happened and try to comfort myself. And ease the pain of exile under this unfamiliar sky.

What causes fourteen-year-old Tariro to leave the home she loves so much?

And how is her fate entwined with that of Katie, another fourteen-year-old who loses her family farm in Zimbabwe in 2000?

Far From Home *is the tense and gripping story of how two girls, though separated by race and time, are destined to play their own part in Zimbabwe's turbulent history.*

**Also for teens,
by Na'ima B. Robert**

from Somalia, with love

Na'ima B. Robert

From Somalia, with love

My name is Safia Dirie. My family has always been my mum, Hoyo, and my two older brothers, Ahmed and Abdullahi. I don't really remember Somalia – I'm an East London girl. But now Abo, my father, is coming to live with us after 12 long years. How am I going to cope?

Safia knows there will be changes ahead, but nothing has prepared her for the reality of dealing with Abo's cultural expectations, her favourite brother Ahmed's wild ways and the temptation of her cousin Firdous's party-girl lifestyle. Safia must come to terms with who she is – as a Muslim, as a poet, as a teenager, as a friend, and, most of all, as a daughter to the father she has never known. Safia must find her own place in the world, so that both father and daughter can start to build the relationship they long for. *From Somalia, with love* is one girl's quest to discover who she is – a story rooted in Somali and Muslim life, that will strike a chord with teenagers everywhere.

Praise for *From Somalia, with Love*

"A unique book that shows the richness
of Somali culture."
School Library Journal

"What will hold readers most are the elemental
questions about the meaning of home."
Booklist

"Has relevance for anybody affected by
frictions between age and group loyalties.
That must include all of us."
Books for Keeps

"Warm, engaging and intensely
thought-provoking..."
Carousel

Read more reviews and extracts at
www.somalialove.com

Na'ima B. Robert is descended from
Scottish Highlanders on her father's side
and the Zulu people on her mother's side.
She was born in Leeds, brought up in Zimbabwe,
and went on to university in London. At High
School her loves included the performing arts,
public speaking, and writing stories that
shocked her teachers!

Her debut novel for teens was warmly
received by reviewers. *School Librarian* said:
"The strong story of Safia's quest to discover
who she is will strike a resonance with many
of today's teenagers." Her picture book
Ramadan Moon, with Shirin Adl, was also
enthusiastically received. "With its flowing text
and striking illustrations, it captures the
excitement and ethos that underlie the
principles of Ramadan." (*Books for Keeps*)

Na'ima divides her time between London and Cairo,
and dreams of living on a farm with her own horses.
Until then she is happy to be a mum to her
four children, and to keep reading and writing books
that take her to a different world each time.

Find out more about what she's up to by visiting
www.naimabrobert.co.uk